The

Foreign

Engagement

SEAN SCOTT KERNS

This book is a work of fiction. Names, characters, places, and incidents either are products of the author's imagination or are used fictitiously. Any resemblance to actual events or locals, or persons, living or dead, is entirely coincidental.

Library of Congress Number 002047689

ISBN: *0991054644*
ISBN-13:978-991054640

DEDICATION

For Audria, Edith, Joseph, Ruby, Carlise

Henderson, Jesse, Geneva, Lloyd,

Edward, and the rest of their crew.

Thank you for setting the example of how

to be a close knit and great family.

CONTENTS

ACKNOWLEDGMENTS

A special thanks to Norman, Denise,

Tony, Tanya and Katrina for their

technical support. Another big thanks to

my content editor, proofreader and

mentor Clarissa.

1

Medicine and Moves

The first order of business was to move Mychal back in the house. Though she was sleeping at home every night, her personal things were still at Luis and Ruby's house. Mychal did not realize she had moved so much stuff from the house during their breakup. She did have help from her ever present wingman, Tony, who complained when he dropped off the items at the university.

The whole process of getting her completely back at home was not moving fast enough for Richard, regardless of his illness. He attempted to help her pack boxes for a few days, overexerted himself, and had to be driven home under protest. Luis tried his best to keep Richard busy and away from Mychal and Ruby, using logic to convince him that not only was he still weak from his current cold, but also that he needed to stay away from Mychal until he could see his doctor. But Richard would not be deterred in his mission. On the last day of boxing Mychal's personal items, he tried to help Mychal pack up clothing and books.

"Honey, please don't help," Mychal pleaded.

Sweaty and flushed, Richard tried to argue, "You are very pregnant and I will not have you packing or moving anything."

"I am not moving an elephant-"she stopped as Richard launched into a coughing spell. "See, that's what I mean. Not only are you in the way, you are also in danger of giving me and the baby whatever crud you have now."

Richard looked hurt before being overtaken by another coughing spell.

Ruby tried to reason with him, "Dearheart, you are miserable. Although I know your heart is in the right place, your head is not. Luis needs to give you something nonprescription for that cough. Luis, Richard needs something for that nasty cough and some rest. Do we have something in the house?"

"I will check the-" Luis started.

"I know we do not have any medicine in the house that would help him.

I think you two should ride to the drugstore to pick something up. The one by the university because they know you by name," Ruby tried throwing a hint to her husband to get Richard out of their way.

Luis appeared confused at first. Richard coughed a few more times. Exacerbated, Ruby finally said a little more forcefully, "Take him to get anything over the counter until he can get to his own physician."

She could see the proverbial light bulb go off over her husband's head. Luis said to Richard, "Come on *hijo*. Let's get you some medication to break up that cough."

Too sick to protest, Richard kissed the top of Mychal's head and followed the older man out the door. When the door closed, the older woman said, "I thought they would never leave."

Both women laughed. Ruby, folding Mychal's sweater, said, "How are your legal troubles? I have not heard you talk about that situation since Richard's proposal."

Mychal sighed, "I seem to have legal troubles everywhere. I finally called those detectives to give them my side of the 'I did not attack Richard's ex-girlfriend' story."

"And?"

"Case closed. No further investigation needed."

"She is *más allá de la locura*. What was Richard ever thinking when he dated that one?" Moving on, Ruby asked, "How about at home?"

Mychal sighed again, "Well, after my brother-in-law made bail the first time, he was arrested again for trying to enter his office, a crime scene. This time when he made bond, he was ordered to surrender his passport. He has changed attorneys and is waiting for a preliminary hearing. I think the prosecutor is gathering more evidence to support that he knowingly defrauded the government. My mother is trying to be strong for everybody including me, but she is a wreck. My oldest brother Max has kept me grounded through this fiasco. Although he is an attorney, he really wants to keep his hands out of the whole mess. My sister-in-law Gwen is trying to keep things normal for their and Reese's kids. People who know the family from the neighborhood are talking. Then there's my baby brother Reese who is trying not to beat up Jake for putting the family through all of this embarrassment. My sister Riley is doing what she does best, being a drama queen that needs all the attention."

"So, no news for or against you?"

"No, not at this point. That's not to say that during further investigation evidence won't come up. Richard said two officials from the embassy called checking to see if I was at the university. He lied, hoping to throw them off. I . . . I," Mychal lost her voice to tears. She sat for a minute, eyes closed and hot tears streaming down her cheeks.

Ruby went to hug her. "I know it's hard."

"I feel so naïve and stupid!" Mychal cried, "I should have asked more questions. I should have been more involved in . . . in whatever he was doing. Now my mother is worried sick. I feel so helpless being away from my family in another country in my own mess."

"Mychal, we mothers are stronger than you think. I remember when our middle son Joseph went through his legal troubles. He was so young and impressionable that he joined a group of boys that sold acquired things. Or at least that is what he told us. They were selling stolen goods. Whether he knew or not, it broke my heart and put his father to shame." Ruby's words faded as if reflecting on the memories stole her voice.

She seemed to snap back and said, "It was a tough time. We blamed ourselves and how we raised him. But in the end, we realized he was an adult, just like your brother-in-law. And just like us, you have to realize there was nothing you could have done. If you were all nosey and more involved, he would have hidden what he was doing better. Then you would not have known the truth and still been in trouble, totally ignorant of the facts."

Mychal's tears dried up listening to Ruby. She had no idea their son had been in any legal trouble. Their three children were young adults with one in college, one studying abroad, and one working. Without thinking she blurted out, "What happened to your son Ruby? What happened in his case?"

The older woman sighed, "He got off light with seven years, four on parole and three in prison. Two of those years were spent in a transitional program. Now, Joseph lives in Barcelona working with the mentally ill population. It taught him a lesson and he was a little more grounded after everything settled."

"Thank you for sharing Ruby,"

Mychal replied softly.

"Well, I did it to let you know although she is worried, your mother will be fine. When you are a mother, I mean beyond this phase, you too will understand." Then Ruby changed subjects, "You should splash some water on your face before the men get back. Richard is already sick and concerned about you. I hope Luis brings him back in a better mood. His attitude, like his health, is very terrible at the moment."

Mychal chuckled and went to their powder room to freshen up. With the water running, she did not hear Richard and Luis return. When she walked into the kitchen, she only saw Luis. "Where's Richard?"

"With my wife loading the boxes in his car. Take him home and put him to bed. Please. He dozed off on the ride back. We got something off the shelf for his cold, but he really needs to see his personal physician. I think it is more than a bad cough."

"Thanks Luis," Mychal hugged him.

Luis hugged back, "Until we know what he has, it is best to limit the exchange of body fluids, if you get my meaning. Also, don't forget to tell your OB about being exposed to some type of sickness."

"I will. My first appointment is next Wednesday."

Luis gave her a scolding look, "Mychal, why did you wait so late? You should have seen a doctor when I first told you in January."

She made her own face, trying to look innocent, "I know, but things blew up and I lived with you, my doctor, so I just put it off."

"Who is it?"

"Dr. Narine. Her office is close to the university."

"Never heard the name. Must be new in the area. Mychal please do not delay any more visits and continue with the prenatal vitamins. Even someone young and healthy like you needs adequate prenatal care," Luis looked aggravated.

"Yes sir," she saluted.

"Mychal. Mychal," Ruby called, "please come and drive this man home. I have taken the keys because he is being difficult."

"See you at work."

"Right to bed when he gets home,"

Luis called after her.

When she went outside Richard and Ruby stood facing each other, arms crossed and looking like both were ready to engage in a battle of wills. Without skipping a beat, Mychal hugged Ruby, took the keys and shot at Richard, "Get in the car."

Before he could protest, she slid in the driver's seat, adjusted the position and started the car. He resigned and plopped in the passenger seat. Mychal did not want to get into any type of argument on the way home. She was glad he dozed off again. Instead of parking in the garage, she parked in the circular drive in the front of the house. When Mychal turned off the car, Richard woke up. In a stern voice she said, "Okay sir, upstairs with you. My doctor said to put you straight to bed."

"*Bella*, we have to get you moved in.

I am fine really," Richard lied.

Mychal looked at him stretched out on the front seat still in work clothes, hair damp from sweating in his sleep and eyes puffy with dark circles. His nose and upper lip were red from over blowing his nose and his chest moved up and down rapidly, indicating shallow breathing. "Really Richard? Really? You look like death buckled in the passenger seat of a sapphire blue Bentley and you are trying to convince me otherwise? There should be a gap in your front teeth as wide as the windshield from that lie you just told."

He chuckled, which caused a coughing spell.

In a tone that inferred she meant business, Mychal said, "You better go upstairs and get in bed or I will not stay."

Richard shot her a dirty look but obeyed, grumbling under his breath in Castilian Spanish. With Mychal following, he went in the front door and straight upstairs to their room. In minutes he was showered, in pajama bottoms and in bed. She went to get him soup, medicine and juice. When Mychal came back, he was on his laptop checking emails.

"No work," she chirped out.

"It is just a message about a shipping order. *Bella*, you did not have to fix me anything. We could have called Pedro's wife, Carmen, to fix something," he took the tray from her.

"They are not here. We discussed using the staff for less daily, simple stuff and more household things. Besides, I need to practice for my duties as your wife," Mychal beamed.

Richard smiled back. He really wanted to take her in his arms and celebrate, but he was too weak and tired for that. Instead he placed his hand on her abdomen, "How is our *niño*?"

"What if it's not a boy? You eat and stop trying to change the subject."

Richard ate until his medicine kicked in. Groggily, he begged Mychal to stay. Against her better judgment, she slipped off her jeans and crawled in bed with him.

They spent the next week doing the same routine, Richard falling asleep and Mychal going to sleep in the guest room closest to the back stairs. Friday he went to his physician alone, not wanting to expose Mychal to people in the waiting room. He stopped by her office with his diagnosis.

"Pneumonia, bacterial type,"

Richard said perching on his favorite spot on her desk, this time no papers.

"How did you get pneumonia?" Before he could answer, she answered her own question, "Let me guess, being stubborn and not taking care of yourself. Or was it overexerting yourself moving boxes and trying to go to work?"

"Funny. Could be one, could be none. I am not sure. The good news is I have some antibiotics and I am past the period of possibly being contagious," he pulled Mychal in his arms and rested his forehead on hers. "I have wanted to do this for weeks. You feel so good right now. I have noticed how you changed. Your breast are so round and your bottom is-"

"Richard!" Mychal blushed, "behave."

"I wonder do you taste the same," ignoring her comment, he kissed her neck. Then he dipped his head to kiss her throat as she tilted her head back. He moved her hips to brush the knot in his jeans, making Mychal moan his name.

"Yeah, everything here tastes the same," he kissed the narrow valley her cleavage created. "What did your doctor say about us, you know, doing us stuff and effecting the baby."

"I didn't ask because I cancelled my appointment."

Richard stopped and stared at Mychal, "What?"

She looked away and said quickly, "I rescheduled it until after your doctor visit. I wanted you to go to the first appointment with me."

Richard cupped her face and brought their eyes to meet. Though his green eyes telegraphed his love, his voice tone was stern, "I love your thoughtfulness, but do not ever do that again. When is your new appointment?"

"Tuesday morning."

"Well until Tuesday morning, no Richard for you."

Mychal looked at him flabbergasted, "Are you serious?"

"Yes *Bella*. This weekend you can sleep with me and I will hold you," he teased.

Mychal pouted, "That's not fair."

"It most definitely is. I went to my appointment and you should have gone to yours. Baby first from now on. But for

27

thinking of me, you get a kiss." Richard pecked her on the lips.

"Go home so I can go to work," she grumbled as she took note of his wide receiver build in smug fitting jeans and a royal blue t-shirt. As he walked toward the door, she said, "It's not right to get a woman all hot and bothered and leave her."

"Your fault," he called over his shoulder.

True to his word, Richard did not attempt to seduce Mychal all weekend. However, he was unbearable to everyone else. Feeling better but limited, he wanted Mychal's clothing and personal items back in their room. Her suitcases and boxes of clothes and personal items were in every unused bedroom upstairs. Richard decided against hiring a moving service for logical

28

and selfish reasons: One his immune system was still on antibiotics and he did not want to come in contact with new germs. And two he did not want strangers moving their personal items. He also decided last minute to make changes to the dynamics of the house. Richard waited until breakfast to bring up his ideas.

"I am considering opening the *suegra* wing of the house. Our family is growing, and I think we, Mychal and I, will need the space."

"Are we moving again?' Mychal asked. "Ruby and Luis are coming today to merge us into one bedroom."

"No, that part of the house will be converted into an apartment for my siblings. I am moving completely into our bedroom and my old room will become the baby's room. I am turning the guest room between my room and Tony's room into my new office. My old office will become my sister's new music room."

"I finally get a more secluded place to practice music and my own apartment? *Gracias a Dios en el cielo!* No more Susanna on display. Now I can try new things and new instruments," his sister threw up her hands in mock exaggeration.

Richard frowned, "What's wrong with playing for the family? You play exceptionally well."

"Richard, I did those formal recitals when I was a child. I am 23 years old," she gave a sad smile. "It really reminds me of Mama and Papa."

With his own nostalgic smile, he said, "I miss them too. I think I will miss them more than ever once my own child is here."

Mychal sat a little uncomfortable but intrigued. Without thinking, she blurted out, "Tell me about them."

Richard and Susanna took turns talking about their parents. Richard talked about how well respected his family was and how their parents were honorable. Susanna contributed funny stories about holidays and her monthly recitals that their parents loved and gave them a chance to show off their only daughter. Richard laughed sadly, adding his own account of the stories but making sure to tell how his job was to keep a mischievous Tony from ruining her recitals. Toward the end of their reminiscing, Tony came in wearing the same clothes from the previous day. Hearing them talk about his parents, he joined in with more stories. Before they realized, the morning was gone, announced by the ringing of the doorbell. Richard answered the door while Susanna cleared the table and Tony went to shower.

Mychal greeted Ruby and Luis. Walking them upstairs she said, "Richard is getting over pneumonia and I have not seen my doctor. I cancelled my appointment so he could go to our first baby appointment. He is boycotting me and will probably try to convince you two how unreasonable I was. Don't be mad or take his side, I was just thinking of his feelings if he missed that milestone first appointment."

Ruby just shook her head, "Mychal, how thoughtful of you to be thoughtless."

"You guys, don't act like that."

Ruby gave her a hug, "Come on dearheart; let's get this move over with so another one of your excuses can be removed from you doing the right thing."

Team Moving Mychal worked out well at first. Richard, Tony and Luis created a system to move Mychal's furniture in the hallway clearing the space for Richard's bedroom set. The heavy dark furniture had more drawer space than hers. When they broke for lunch, it was decided that they would break down Richard's bed and move it into their room. Mychal remained quiet not wanting to express her true thoughts. When the group went to start the afternoon task, she stayed to clean up. Mychal heard Richard coughing, announcing his presence in the kitchen.

"*Bella*, you are quiet. What's wrong? Do not lie and say 'nothing' because I know you."

"Nothing," Mychal did not look up from the refrigerator.

"Talk to me."

Mychal turned to face Richard, "I guess I am tired."

Richard broke into another coughing spell. It took some seconds before he replied, "You are a terrible liar. You were fine all day until I talked about moving my bed into our room."

"What's wrong with our bed we have now?" she whined.

"What is wrong with the bed that goes with the set?" he questioned back.

"Because she slept with you there," Mychal shot back.

Richard's face changed to register slight frustration, "*Mi Dios Bella* is that what caused this sudden mood swing, my past with Demitri again."

"No! Well yes. Richard, have you noticed we have never done anything in your bed or even in your room?" His reply was an open palm shrug. "Never noticed? Not once? Well the whole time we dated, she slept in your room. Now that she is gone, I let you fall asleep in our bed and I slept in the guest room beside your room."

Richard's face finally registered recognition of her point, "Mychal come on, you know that is silly. You already said you were over it around the holidays."

"I am!"

"I cannot tell by the temper tantrum you are throwing right now," raising his voice caused Richard to cough a few more times.

"Well, I can't sleep there knowing that you once shared that bed with her doing whatever. The woman tried to break us up. She wanted me to end my pregnancy. I don't want those thoughts resurfacing every time I get in bed. If you *must* know, *that* is what I have been dealing with ever since you came up with that brilliant idea this morning," Mychal folded her arms across her chest.

"So, you are not okay with that being the baby's room either, are you?" he frowned.

"I didn't say that. I know that has been your room since childhood and you want our child to have that room. A priest and a fresh coat of paint will work wonders," Mychal quipped.

"Okay. Okay. Will a new bed solve this problem?" Richard conceded.

"Yes," Mychal took a deep breath,

"yes it will."

"Can I keep my furniture?" he teased. "I hate for all this work to be done in vain. I think if we tell that group they have to move stuff back, they might revolt."

"Absolutely, as long as you did not do anything bizarre on it. I'm not a total control freak."

"Nice to know," Richard croaked, then coughed.

"Take some medicine, you sound horrible," she ordered.

"Control freak."

"Rebel."

"*Dios*, I want you right now." Richard pulled her in his arms and kissed her tenderly on the lips. His kiss left her mouth to taste the hollow of her neck and onto her growing cleavage. "I love this upgrade. Can we keep them?"

Mychal giggled, "Come on, people are waiting on us."

When they walked up the stairs, the quartet of Susanna, Tony, Ruby and Luis were waiting. Tony spoke first, "Is the fight over?"

"We were not fighting," Mychal started then switched subjects. "I was trying to get Richard to take his cough medicine. I think he overdid it. Again."

"If he is coughing more than earlier, probably so. Go get well *mi hijo*. We got this. Doctor's orders," Luis instructed.

Mychal gave Richard a smug look and received a swat on the behind.

The women pulled drawers out of

Richard's furniture to make it lighter so the men could put it on the dolly and move it. With most of the heavy lifting done, Tony, Luis and a drugged Richard moved her old furniture in his old room then created a makeshift conveyor line to move Mychal's things back into their room. Clothing, pictures, books and boxes of personal items took the rest of the afternoon to get somewhere in or around their room. Richard looked spacey and appeared to be in the way at times. Between moving all the furniture around, Susanna came to Mychal with an overly exacerbated look.

"Get him!" she almost yelled at Mychal. "He is in the way!"

Mychal pulled Richard into their living room and talked about the timeline for decorating the baby's room. They talked about her appointment on Tuesday so the others could finish up. Midway through the conversation, Richard fell asleep, his medicine finally taking effect. With Richard out of the way and his bedroom furniture arranged without the drawers in their room, Mychal, Ruby and Susanna talked while moving clothes and shoes into the room.

"So Mychal, have any wedding ideas yet?" Ruby asked.

"Ruby, I really have not put much thought in it. I do know I want something small given my current situation."

The older woman stopped moving socks and stared at Mychal. "Okay, I am tired of hearing that excuse. Mychal you are not the first pregnant woman with difficult circumstances and you will not be the last. Stop looking at yourself as some sort of victim. This should be the best time of your life. Quit looking at the proverbial glass as half empty. I told you this before, stop being afraid of your past. Enjoy the man that loves you because he deserves it and you do too."

"I agree," Susanna slid two drawers in place. "My brother deserves happiness. We already love you like family. We need to get busy planning to make it official."

Mychal blinked back the moisture behind her eyes. She cleared her throat before saying, "I'm sorry to be an emotional basket case. I do love Richard and I have been secretly thinking about my wedding plans. I only got as far as picking you two as bridesmaids along with my sister."

Susanna broke into a broad grin and Ruby replied, "I would be honored."

"Great," Mychal got up, "ladies, I am tired of moving. Let's find some food."

Later that evening Mychal was on her laptop when Richard walked into their living room toweling his hair. "So what else have you planned for our wedding other than bridesmaids?"

"I thought you were asleep."

"I was napping. I heard Ruby too. She is right, you deserve an official wedding. Let me know what your heart desires and I will make it happen."

Mychal's heart swelled with emotions. She stored her computer and motioned for him to join her. Richard complied but was puzzled when she directed him to sit on the floor after she kissed him. Slowly Mychal dried his hair, gently massaging his scalp. His position was not lost on her; this was as close as they had been in weeks other than falling asleep together. Though they talked about which family members to invite, she felt tiny shocks every time he brushed her leg or shifted to get more comfortable. Richard noticed he was doing all the talking. He shifted to look at Mychal, whose amber eyes telegraphed her burning need.

"Oh no. You have not been to the doctor. Our deal-" the rest of what he had to say was smothered in her kiss. Despite his mind saying no, his body responded to her aggressiveness, which always added to his excitement. Caught in an awkward position both physically and mentally, Richard had no time to make a decision before Mychal slid to his level and positioned herself to straddle him. She rocked against his lap while trailing kisses from his ear to his chin.

"Mychal, we need to . . . " was all he could manage before she captured his mouth again. That broke his resolve. His hands seemed to catch fire, first kneading her slightly engorged breast under her shirt then working their way inside the waist band of her yoga pants.

Knowing she finally got him where she wanted him, Mychal raised to her knees long enough to pull her pants down and slip his pants over his hips. Richard, her willing accomplice, kicked off his pajama pants the rest of the way then yanked her shirt and pants completely off with the skill of a magician performing a classic table trick. Barriers gone, Mychal eased on Richard inch by inch enjoying the sound of his breath catching. At once she thrust down hard taking him by surprise.

"Mi Dios Bella," Richard threw his head back.

At that reaction, Mychal did it again and again, watching his body buck and twist each time. Richard was between enjoying this torture and wanting to release. He pulled his legs up in a low wide V and braced Mychal against his thighs. He controlled her movement while tasting her neck. She continued his set pace as his thumbs massaged the apex of her overgrown breast. Mychal arched her back and moaned loudly at the added pleasure of this new sensation Richard was causing. Loving her response, he replaced his thumbs with his mouth, taking his time tasting each one. With Richard's hands on her hips guiding her and his mouth driving her crazy, Mychal dug her fingers in his hair and cried out his name before losing herself in her own quivering movements.

Richard released Mychal to watch the results of his handiwork. She was so beautiful to him in her current raw emotional state. Before he could register,

Mychal pulled him into a kiss that conveyed she was not done. Her pace increased while her mouth tasted everywhere on his face, neck, jawline and back to his mouth. Richard grabbed Mychal in a tight embrace, thrusting against her hips and swearing in Castilian Spanish. His legs dropped followed by intermediate spasms. Neither moved for what seemed an eternity. Realizing he might be mashing her abdomen, Richard moved to lay them on the floor. She leaned in to rest her head on his shoulder.

"*Bella*, that was amazing. Is this some new pregnancy thing?" he teased making circles on her solid midriff.

"Nope, I just missed you. All of you," Mychal snuggled closer.

"Come on, into bed with you," Richard got up and pulled Mychal to her feet. "And no more of any overexerting activities until Tuesday. Promise?"

"Promise? Um, yeah," She tossed back. No sooner had he turned off the lamp than Mychal broke that promise.

2
Complications and Visitations

Mychal's first visit to her obstetrician was an experience for both she and Richard. They sat in a moderate sized waiting room filling out the necessary forms amidst a few other pregnant women. A couple of times Richard nuzzled her neck and whispered things like 'can't believe we are going to be parents' and 'can't wait to kiss your belly'. Mychal could not help but giggle like a schoolgirl. Though he could not be with her for labs, he could come in the examination room.

Mychal's doctor was a petite older woman from Ghana named Irene Narine. Her native accent was evident even in her English which had British undertones. Her chocolate eyes were warm as she spoke, but her message was clear: from this point forward Mychal was to follow all doctor recommendations to ensure the health of mother and child. When Mychal was sketchy on possible date of conception, measurements and an ultrasound were performed to determine she was 18 weeks. Both she and Richard were in awe at the image on the screen. Richard squeezed her hand hearing the baby's heartbeat for the first time.

"I cannot go back to work after this," he blurted out. "I have to celebrate or buy baby stuff."

Dr. Narine laughed and reminded him he would have several more visits like this one. She printed a picture from the ultrasound for them to take home. Both were so excited they forgot to ask about the sex of the baby. After a few more minutes of discussion, Mychal left with a new prenatal vitamin prescription and a schedule of appointments leading up to a due date in the second week of August, two weeks after Mychal's birthday. Richard left with a book for expecting fathers and answers about intimacy during the pregnancy.

On the way to her office they were giddy and silly. A soon as she got to campus, Mychal got ready for her twelve o'clock class. At her break, Richard called to say he needed to stay late at work due to an expensive shipping problem. He was sending Tony to pick her up after five. As soon as Mychal disconnected the call, Demitri appeared in her door like an unwanted apparition.

"Mychal."

"Go away before I call security," Mychal began to feel warm from anger.

Demitri held up her hands in surrender, "Wait, I am not here for that."

"Then why are you here?"

"To apologize. To make things right between us," the other woman sounded earnest.

"Honestly Demitri, I do not think that will ever, ever happen. You dug up my past, threatened my family, and wanted my pregnancy terminated. To make matters worse, you lied and accused me of assault and attempted murder. There is no 'making things right' comeback from that!" Mychal was so angry she was getting loud.

A wave of nausea made her stomach lurch.
The unpleasant sensation quenched her
temper. She sat down, not even realizing
she had stood up. Slightly calmer she said,
"However, if it will make you leave, I half
ass accept your half ass apology. Now you
can leave before I give you a real reason to
call the police."

There was a brief silence before
Demitri broke out in a cold voice, "It did
not have to come to this at all. I just wanted
Richard to see you for the *capulina* that you
are. Thanks to you, he not only ended our
relationship, but also our friendship. That
hurt beyond anything he could have
physically done."

For a moment Mychal felt sorry for
her. Richard was more than her husband-
to-be, he was her best friend too and losing
him would make her feel the same way the
other woman was feeling now. She said

almost apologetically, "Demitri that was his choice. Richard has been busy and did not mention he talked with you. I did not know anything about that until now."

"I do not believe you," Demitri spat back.

"Dr. Ayscue, *está todo bien?*" one of the graduate assistants poked his head out into the hallway.

Mychal recognized his voice. "I'm fine Giovanni, just leaving for class."

She turned to Demitri, patience thinning and said, "You don't have to believe me. Either way I don't give a damn. I have a class to teach. Don't ever come to my office again or you will hope security can get here before I give you a real reason to file some charges."

The other woman's answer was a

nasty look.

"Get the hell out," Mychal took a step toward the door, soft briefcase in hand, "because as far as I'm concerned we can start on those reasons right now."

Without another word Demitri exited the room in a dramatic theater fashion.

Mychal was still irritated at the end of the day when Tony picked her up in his new metallic pearl Maserati coupe.

"How was your day?" The younger man flashed her a broad grin. He was as handsome as Richard, just slimmer. Where Richard had a more solid wide receiver build, his brother Tony was a bit wirier in build. Almost identical in height, as well as green eye color, Tony wore his raven colored hair shorter, highlighted and gelled in various styles. While Richard dressed in khakis or slacks and polo shirts, his brother was always outfitted in jeans and a super tight shirt that showed off his well-toned torso. Mychal could see why he always had a new girl.

"Cool. I'm really pregnant and I had a crazy visitor," she sighed.

"Who? One of my exes?" Tony joked.

"No, your brother's."

At first he was silent, clearly perplexed then said, "Not her. Connie I would believe, but not Demitri. *Carajo! Maldita sea, espero que rompe su cuello!*"

"Hey, hey, English Uncle Tony. Richard is not going to break anybody's neck because we are not going to tell him. He is dealing with enough right now."

"Doc, you know I am down for the cause, but I do not think that is a good idea," he sounded skeptical.

"At this point I believe it is the best recourse. I handled it my way so if she had any common sense, she won't come back," she tried to sound flippant.

"Again, I don't know. Let me think about it."

They rode the rest of the way making small talk about the changes taking place around the house.

Tony turned down the driveway to the house and finally said, "Mychal, I am not sure about this not telling Ricardo business. *Mi hermano* will be furious if he finds out we kept something this important from him."

Mychal waited until Tony parked

the car and said, "Listen, today's pointless visit can wait. Richard just got back to work in the last two weeks after being out sick. Also, there is some crisis that obviously needs his attention to the degree he needed you to pick me up. This Demitri thing is not a problem that needs to compete with his other problems right now. I will take measures to make sure this does not happen again and let him know what happened by the weekend. So ease your conscience, I got this."

Tony shook his head, "I do *not* like this Doc. You already saw what happened when you kept things from him in the past. For the record, I am not moving anything else to, from, or within this house."

Richard came home while Mychal was lying in bed dozing off. He tried not to wake her but did while showering. When she tried to get him to talk about work, he mentioned a few things then changed the subject to the baby. His mood lightened up as they discussed names. Richard fell asleep in Mychal's arms, his safe place from the rest of the world.

Mychal waited until after midterms to talk with campus security about Demitri. She tried to keep it quiet, but her dean got involved. If her contract was renewed at the end of the semester, her office would be moved. Knowing this would snowball out of her control to upper administration, Mychal called Richard who answered almost immediately with, "Is the baby okay?"

Mychal sighed, "Yes, the baby is fine. What are you doing for lunch?"

"Trying to break the surface of this sea of paperwork on my desk."

"Want lunch in your office?"

Richard laughed, "With my future wife and son or daughter, anytime. How about seafood?"

She sighed again, loving his good mood and hating to be the rain cloud on it. "Sounds great honey. Get me blackened fish and seasoned veggies. I am hungry today."

"I will have Morcheeba order it and by the time you get here, the food will have arrived."

Instead of her usual racecar pace, Mychal drove the Porsche slower than normal to his office while rehearsing what and how to tell him about the incident in a way that would not set Richard off the deep end. When she got to his office, his conference table already held their lunch. Richard, dressed in a navy blue suit, no jacket, no vest and periwinkle blue shirt with the sleeves rolled up, sat at his desk on the phone. His handsome face was sporting a deep scowl.

When he saw her Richard completely lost his train of thought. Mychal had eased in his office so quietly, she might as well have floated in. Her rust colored dress was hanging on every curve and made her no longer flat abdomen appear slightly pronounced. The hem of her dress brushed inches above her knees, showing off Mychal's toned legs made extra sexy by black peep toe pumps. Richard's mouth suddenly became dry and he knew what he needed. Phone call almost forgotten, he said, "Gabriel, *voy a seguir esta llamada después del almuerzo.*"

Next, he called his secretary to ask her to hold his calls and not to disturb him. Richard met Mychal in the middle of his office and kissed her. He kissed her like she was gone for months, his hands feeling all of her growing curves. His mouth left hers only to taste the hollow of her neck.

"Richard, I missed you too. But honey what if someone walks into your office and sees us?"

With a great deal of frustration, he left her embrace to lock the door then returned to sweep her over to the small bar beside his bathroom. Richard kissed her neck while his hands worked on his belt. Mychal knew something was wrong when he was on the phone. His actions spoke volumes that he needed her right now, physically and mentally. Whatever Richard needed she would give without a second thought, to ease his mind and his tension.

He freed himself then worked off her bikinis. He pulled her to the very edge of the bar and joined them in graceless movements. Mychal wrapped her legs around his waist and wordlessly urged him to continue. Fueled by passionate urgency, Richard set a tempo that resulted in both their explosive yet quiet releases. Spent, Richard pulled her into a tight embrace and kissed her hair. He joked in her ear, "I am making it official that you cannot come to my office looking that sexy again."

Mychal stroked his face, "That was not me. That was all you. What's wrong? Talk to me."

Richard sighed, "Let's clean up and eat. I will tell you."

Over lunch Richard told Mychal the current issues at work. When he was home battling his cold, a few accidents happened at the port to his ship. This past week a shipment of imported American trucks was damaged the night the ship docked. Richard had to deal with the insurance company on each incident but wanted to do some investigating on his own. He wanted to hire an assistant before the baby was born so he could work from home. Mychal suggested Tony.

"*Bella* be serious. Tony is *a mujeriego y un sinvergüenza* and is not committed to anything in life. I mean other than his conquest of women. I need an assistant to actually help me and not require babysitting," Richard finished his lunch.

"Give him a chance. He is smarter than you give him credit for," she threw back.

"Smart, yes. Devoted to something other than his lifestyle, no." He changed the subject, "So what was so important you wanted to see me for lunch?"

Mychal looked away nervously.

"What is it? The baby?"

"No, I had a visitor on campus some time ago. I was uncomfortable and spoke with security. It was no big deal-"

She was cut off by Richard, "Security? Do not sit there and say it is no big deal if security was involved. You start talking right now, from the beginning. When did this happen?"

"Last week or so. . . ish" Mychal mumbled.

"Last week! Mychal, you are so . . ." the rest of what he said sounded like angry Castilian Spanish profanity.

"Richard, I was trying to handle it.

64

Plus, you had all that stuff happening at work. I could tell you were preoccupied," she tried to explain.

"Mychal, that is not good enough. I just told you about the mess here at work, while you kept something else from me yet again. Plain and simple," Richard was really aggravated.

"I know and I am sorry. I was just trying to . . ." her words failed. She looked away, trying to contain her tears.

Damn. The last thing he wanted to do was make her cry. Richard took Mychal's hand and kissed her palm. "Calm down. We will work through this if you just tell me everything. Do they at least know who it is?"

Mychal looked away again and said, "Yes, they have an idea."

Puzzled he tried again, "So do you know the person?"

She shook her head affirmative.

"Dammit woman, who is it?"

Mychal took a sip of tea and mumbled in her glass, "Demitri."

"What? It almost sounded like you said Demitri," he gave her a narrowed eyed, disbelieving look.

Finally, she faced him and said, "I did but don't go off the deep end. Security has this under control. And you know I can protect myself."

Richard gave her a hard look, "Are you done yet? What did she say?"

Mychal took a breath, "She wanted to apologize. She wanted to make things right. I told her there was no 'making things right'. She accused me of making you cut her off from your interestingly dysfunctional friendship. She said she missed you and I ordered her out.

"Is that all?"

"Yes honey, I promise," she wiped her eyes from the tears that threatened to spill out.

"Okay," he got up and pulled her into his arms, rocking her in their embrace. "It is okay. We will handle this. Go back to work. I will see you at home."

Mychal looked up at her soon to be husband with relief. Richard kissed her tenderly before saying, "No more lunches in my office for you."

"Again, that was your fault," she smiled.

"Actually, it was yours. I love you, now go back to work. I will be home later than usual."

Mychal covered her disappointment by pulling away, "I love you too. Hurry home."

"As long as you have my heart, I will always hurry home," was the last thing she heard him say before walking out the door.

Richard dug into his work with new vigor. Long after the staff left, he finished his audit of the damage done by the most recent unfortunate event. Before snapping off the desk lamp, he contacted his personal attorney.

"Señor Nuaze-Piedra, how are you my fine gentleman?"

"Ricardo, why so formal you old soul?" his lawyer boomed on the other end in perfect English. Henrico Nuaze-Piedra was one of his father's oldest friends, family lawyer and his godfather.

"Well señor, the hour is late and-" Richard began.

"Nonsense! What can I do for you?" the older gentleman interrupted.

"Señor, I need a protection order and or restraining order. I am not sure which," Richard floundered. "Some things are happening right now and I need to protect my fiancée. She is pregnant and-"

The older man cut him off again, "Pregnant fiancée? Look at you all grown up and going to be a papa and a husband. *Hijo de Rohas!* Is it the American professor? I knew she was the one when I met her. You have to tell me when is the wedding. I bet that old bag Solé that it would be less than a year. Your parents would have been so proud."

Richard blushed, feeling like a teenager, "I know. I wish they could have met her. Even with her American ways, she would have won Papa over."

"She did say she was from New York. That is no surprise since you always liked international women. What happened to that Greek girl who was in the theater? I saw her at the holiday party too."

Richard sighed, "That is the problem. I think that she is stalking my fiancée."

Intrigued, his lawyer said, "This sounds a little complicated. Now tell me everything; not as your lawyer, but as your Uncle Rico."

For almost an hour Richard talked

about Mychal and their situation. Talking to his Uncle Rico made him really miss his father. His father would know how to handle Demitri, Mychal's troubles at home, and his current work issues. At the end of their conversation, he felt better. It was decided that tomorrow his uncle would petition one of his judge friends for a protection order for the entire household, including Mychal who was a non-citizen. Mychal's legal problems were now made aware to the right person and he was given advice on how to handle what his lawyer referred to as 'questionable activities' in his company.

Richard drove home ready to see Mychal who was up posting work for her class. They dined together on leftovers for him and ice cream for her. When they went to bed, he slept more soundly than he had in days.

Richard spent the next few weeks at the docks talking with various personnel about the truck shipping issue. His company was shipping a fleet of trucks from Mexico and somehow the trucks where not secured in the containers. When they were unloaded, more than a dozen of the fifty were damaged. While his insurance company investigated, Richard did his own probing. Three weeks prior to this fleet incident a container carrying toys from the Philippines caught on fire and another shipment full of children's clothing was found to have damage from rats. Again, insurance covered the loss, but the whole mess cast doubt on his company. Richard did indeed need help but was still skeptical about putting his little brother in a position to give that help.

Glad for the weekend without work, Richard decided to do something special. First, he invited Mychal to go out for dinner, then told her they needed to do one last errand before going home. For dinner they went to a Mediterranean restaurant on the *Paseo del Prado* then strolled hand in hand to the square at *La Plaza de Cibeles* discussing wedding plans and nursery themes. Richard convinced her to see the statue close up. Once in front of the landmark, he pulled Mychal in his arms and began, "Nothing has been the same since the day you walked into my life."

Mychal hugged him back, "I feel the same way."

"I know *Bella*," Richard pulled away, got down on one knee and pulled a square black box from his pocket. "Mychal

Ayscue, you deserve a formal proposal.
Will you marry me, be my wife and soul
mate or my *alma gemela*?

Mychal looked at his ring nestled in
the black box with the most elegant
diamond she had ever seen in her life. It
was an emerald cut diamond with purple
hues in a white gold setting. Tears slipped
out of her eyes.

"*¿Cuál es tu respuesta señorita?*" a
bystander asked.

That broke her paralysis, "Oh
Richard, you are such an old romantic soul!
Yes. Yesterday, today and tomorrow."

A small crowd of spectators
applauded as Richard slipped the ring on
her finger and rose to kiss her. As he
nuzzled her face Mychal whispered,
"Hopeless romantic."

"Sí, sí mama."

Back at home they spent time looking at wedding venues on the computer before going to bed. Before closing his eyes, Richard's phone buzzed with a message.

> **From Demitri:** I miss you! There will never be another relationship like ours. Can we at least be friends?

> **He sent back:** We cannot be friends after that last stunt you pulled with Mychal. Get on with your life. Never contact us again.

> **She sent:** You will be so sorry. She will not make you happy like I did. I hate you.

Richard turned his phone off and rolled over to snuggle with Mychal.

3
Parents and Drama

Over the weekend, Richard conceded that Mychal's idea about bringing Tony into the business might have some merit. In addition to needing help at work, he also needed Susanna to help with the remodeling project at home. Sunday evening was spent working out details and plans in both areas. By Monday, everybody had their own project: Richard was doing damage control at work, Susanna was meeting with the interior designer, Tony started his official training at the docks and Mychal was working on their wedding.

Mychal's abdomen began to swell to the point she needed new clothes to accommodate her no longer slim waistline. After her twenty-two week appointment, she decided to go shopping. Richard was adamant about going with her. They drove to the outlets where she picked up a few shopping bags of clothes to accommodate her expanding waistline. Over lunch they set a date for the first of June and decided to fly her family over. Mychal had mixed feelings about seeing her family but missed them enough to deal with their peculiar ideas of family togetherness.

Prior to heading to his office, they stopped by her department to pick up some assignments her students left in her mailbox. Richard was at the bookshelf behind her office door when an unexpected visitor arrived. Before Mychal had time to register a thought, Demitri stomped in and started on her, "I thought we let things settle between us. Now you are keeping Richard from answering my calls and-"

"Leave," Mychal cut her off pointing at the hallway, "leave now dammit."

Demitri turned pale to Mychal's puzzlement. "Is that what I think it is?"

"If you are asking," Richard caught both women's attention, "about my fiancée's ring, yes, it is my mother's ring."

Demitri's pale face was marked with a furious scowl, "How could you?"

Richard shot back, "How could I what? Show the world that I was going to marry my fiancée? Not check with you first? Have you forgotten that we were over long before she even boarded the plane to leave New York or are you just slow? And if I were a betting man, I would wager you had some twisted idea that by exposing her past I would come back to you out of hurt and obligation. Did you think I forgot that you wanted to terminate my child? Well, I did not forget that offense, nor did I forgive it. After all that you said and did, I wanted nothing to do with the monster you have become. I am beginning to think that maybe you were a monster the entire time we were together, and I was just in denial."

She looked wounded by his words. A tear escaped her eye and her voice was cracked with emotion when Demitri spoke, "Richard, I was just caught off guard. I . . . I did not mean those things. I just wanted you to see her for the opportunist she really was. I did not mean to hurt you."

"And after that. Going to the authorities and lying about Mychal trying to kill you. What was your point in that move? To have her embarrassed, arrested, or deported carrying my child? *Estás demente*!"

"To expose her. She is a violent woman who threaten me. She almost hit me with a glass! You saw her hit me that night. She is dangerous. I was just trying to get her out of your life for your own safety." The other woman almost pleaded.

"A noble thought. But why would I needed saving from her when she did not do half of the things, I know you have done." Richard's dark green eyes bore into his ex-girlfriend, "It is funny that you think I needed saving. Who saved me from you and your violence?"

Mychal looked back and forth between the two people in her office like a tennis match spectator.

"How could I not know who she really was? Not only did she live in my house but I was in her bed every night," he gave Mychal a teasing wink. "I knew enough to know she was my soul mate and everything I wanted in a wife."

Demitri's face darken with rage and she let out a scream of frustration at his last dig.

"Mychal, was that a scream? Are you alright?" Connie came across the hall to check on her.

"No Connie, call security," Mychal managed to say.

Richard said to Demitri, "This is the last warning you get. Stay away from us. Period. If I see you anywhere near my family again, the authorities will arrest you."

"You will regret this! Both of you! Mark my words!" With that, Demitri brushed past Connie, almost knocking the other woman over as she stormed off.

Connie looked at Demitri then back at Richard and Mychal. Good natured, she said, "Good to see you Richard. Mychal, more drama today?"

Mychal just shook her head in disgust with sagging shoulders. Richard spoke for her, knowing Mychal was speechless. "Thank you, Connie, for your help today. Your intervention was greatly appreciated."

"I got the department email, and I was concerned for her. *Novia*, do not let that crazy woman bother you. The semester will be over in a month and your office will be moved," she offered Mychal a sympathetic smile.

Mychal attempted to smile back, "I hope so."

"It will be fine *novia*, "Connie offered, then walking out said, "Again, good to see you Richard."

In the car leaving his office Mychal was still silent. Richard drove a different route that she assumed was going home. Instead, they turned into a cemetery and drove past a beautiful temple. Mychal continued to stare out the window at tombs and extravagant statues that marked graves. She marveled at people placing flowers and seemingly sitting on chairs by graves. Richard stopped the car and turned to her, "I wish I knew what to say to make things better. I had no idea Demitri would behave this way. *Bella*, I am sorry you even had to go through dealing with my past."

Mychal continued to look out the

window, "It's not that. I wanted to punch her in the face since the day we met. She is so lucky that I am pregnant now. It just seems the more we are together; the more life throws at us. I just don't know. My past, your past, the company issues, everything seems against us. Is it all an omen of some kind?"

"No *Bella*. That is no omen, that is just life. We are starting out a little rough, but remember anything worth having is worth the struggle. When I am dealing with difficulties, I come here to refocus. When you left me, I came here daily just to talk with my parents. Sometimes I came to drink and have a cigar with my father." He finished with a sly smile, "He smoked."

Mychal's heart and stress melted away like snow on a hot car. She turned to give him a tender kiss.

"Come on woman, let's meet my parents." Richard hopped out of the car and came to her side. Together they walked through the vaults until they came to one with the statue of a weeping angel. "Mychal, my parents Rohas Roman and Alejandra Iban."

She was so touched that she squeezed his hand. Richard talked to the gravestones, telling his parents how he and Mychal were having a healthy baby and would be married in seven weeks. He told them about the problems at work and the Demitri situation. Finally, he promised to honor them at his wedding and continue to care for his siblings. When Richard was finished, Mychal hugged him. She felt him exhale against her. Together they walked back to the car in silence. On the way home she broke the silence, "I can't help but wonder if what is happening is some kind of karma. I know I messed up back home, but I don't want my mess to affect you."

"Mychal, the truth is I wanted you long before I knew about your situation. That night at the staff party when you gave me that drunk kiss I knew then I wanted you." He chuckled, "Something about being attacked by you sparked my hope and faith in a normal relationship with an extraordinary person. It gave my injured ego a boost to be desired by a beautiful woman."

Mychal gave him a look of mock astonishment, "I did not attack you."

It was Richard's turn to look astonished, "Yes you did! You had on next to nothing and I was touching your lip. Then, bang, pulled into a kiss and groped like a *súper modelo masculino*."

"Groped!" Mychal laughed. "Not true and you started it with that 'kiss it and make it better' comment. Big flirt, that's what you were."

"Guilty as charged," he laughed with her as they pulled into the driveway. Richard turned to Mychal who was suddenly quiet. "What's wrong?"

She grabbed his hand and put it under her clothes to touch her naked skin, "Feel that?"

It took Richard a minute, but he felt movement beneath his hand. Then, she moved his hand to another spot on her firm abdomen where it felt like water running under her skin. Richard smiled at Mychal with a new wonder, "He is moving."

"Yes, the baby is moving. Probably because I am hungry. That was a weird feeling, like butterflies under my skin."

"Come on, we need to get some food for my son."

"Son," she got out of the car.

"Oh yeah, moving like that it is definitely a boy with the karate kick of his mother," he teased.

"Or a girl, stubborn like her father," Mychal teased back.

"I will love either. Come, time to eat and work on wedding stuff and flights," Richard took her hand and held it like he would never let go.

4

Politics and Sabotage

It was decided that the front lawn would be a great place for a small wedding. It was blooming with flowers in June and could hold around 100 people. Susanna was helping Mychal with finalizing the wedding plans while balancing school and mediating between the designers and Richard. So far the only main house plans that were approved was that the nursery remodel would begin within the next two weeks.

Mychal was dreading to have so

much going on toward the end of the semester. She needed to wrap up the last three major items on her wedding to-do list before exams started. So on the university's study day, she and Susanna took the morning to work on the major wedding matters and tackle the smaller details of the wedding plans starting with decorations. Before lunch the rental company sent over the contract for arches and chairs for Richard to sign. Appointments for caterers were set for the weekend and flight arrangements for her family were confirmed. By the time Richard came home from work, Mychal was tired. Together, they picked colors and talked about how Tony's presence was helping the situation at work.

That night Mychal called home to tell her mother her pre-flight information. Her mother shared that she was receiving calls from an investigator and a lawyer. Her mother was afraid to come to the wedding. Mychal did her best to calm her mother, reassuring her that everything would be fine. She did not know how, but somehow she and Richard would make this work. The conversation switched to the baby and nursery plans. Mychal hung up with her mother feeling even more drained than before the call.

The week of exams was spent grading finals and picking out menus. She was so preoccupied that she forgot an appointment with her department chair, Dr. Gabriel Echevarría. He knocked at her door startling Mychal out of her concentration.

"Dr. Ayscue," his r sounds rolled off his tongue like a cat's purr.

"Dr. Echevarría. Am I in trouble? I

am so sorry about that security thing. I wish I could have avoided that situation all together," her words came out in a rush.

"Señorita, Mychal, slow down," he paused to give her a second. "I am not here about that. I emailed your evaluation and contract two weeks ago. You did not respond. I came in person to see if you had a problem with the evaluation and contract or if you were planning to return as a tenure track professor researcher?"

"I want to, I guess. I mean, I am due a week before the fall semester starts. I didn't really know what to do," she chewed her lip.

"Without getting too personal, what are your plans? I would guess . . . I mean . . . are you going to stay here in the area?" he tried to ask without sounding awkward.

"Oh yes," she was emphatic.

"Great, that saves me the time and cost of advertising that position. My portion of the evaluation is completed in the email. Please complete your part and send it back today, posthaste. It is already late."

"Thank you," Mychal gushed in relief as she rose to shake his hand.

"That will not be necessary. Are you still teaching summer school as per the original contract?"

"Um, yes." She was a little confused, "Dr. Echevarría, why are you asking all of these questions? Of course I will fulfill my contractual obligation. Being pregnant does not allow me any different or special treatment than any other employee in the department."

Echevarría gave her a direct look, "Señorita, you have friends in important places and that is not lost on me. Aside from not wanting to upset your condition, I do not want to upset our department's relationship with the administration."

Mychal did get up then, shaking her head back and forth. "Oh no. No sir. I do not want any favoritism. Do not offer me a job because of Richard, I mean Señor Garçia-Torrés. I do not operate like that. I work on merit and my work speaks for itself."

Her department chair chose his words carefully, "No, that is not what I mean. You are getting the wrong idea. Your work was and is excellent. The students loved your classes and your co-workers had nothing but accolades to say about you. You have proven that you are a capable and solid professional. We have never had a situation where the visiting professor actually stayed on as faculty after their year's contract. The fact that you are family to the chairman is an American win-win situation. We do not have to exert time and money in another candidate search which keeps the chancellor happy who in turn keeps the board happy."

"It sounds like politics," came Mychal's dry retort.

Dr. Echevarría turned to leave, "Politics maybe, good business, yes. Keeping you on as faculty is a good business decision concerning a position that has been difficult to fill in the past. Who you are associated with is an asset for you and you are an asset to me. Take that how you want; I meant no disrespect."

She settled down a bit feeling a little embarrassed, "Sorry. I have been a tad on edge lately."

"*De nada*. But I will not apologize for wanting a published researcher on my team. It makes the department look great." He paused at the door, "Have an inked copy on my desk by Monday. Also pack up your office. Sometime during the two week break I will have facilities management move you to a different office. Remember Dr. Ayscue, grades in by Friday. Good day."

Mychal mentioned her meeting with the department chair Saturday while they were en route to their second catering sample appointment. She joked, "I'm pleased you used your influence to help me."

"Sorry *Bella*, I cannot take credit for that one. Uncle Juan briefed me on that agenda, but I did not attend that meeting. I was going over workers' personnel jackets with Tony," he sighed.

"Don't you employ like a thousand people? What was the reason behind that?" Mychal inquired.

"It is the second level of improving security to prevent these unfortunate and costly mishaps. Mychal, I am so glad I took your suggestion about Tony. He is an astute business protégé. When this mess is over, I am going to turn over a degree of daily operations to him. He is great with people. Tony is so easy and down to earth that he is approachable on every level," Richard finished beaming with a pride that only an older brother could have.

"He very much wanted to help. For your approval he would do any-"

"Well he fooled me," Richard cut

across her. "All he has ever done is party, parade women in and out of his life and waste money."

"The exact opposite of you, Mister Serious. Mister I have to run the family and be the patron. Mister steering the business into my father's true dream. Mister older and wiser brother who knows all and sees all." Mychal was so goofy imitating him with a gruff voice and arms positioned in a mock burly gesture, that Richard could do nothing but laugh. She laughed along with him.

"*No me suena como que,*" he chuckled.

"Yes you do. Always serious and always grumpy."

Richard sighed, "I know I have been a grouch lately. There is a lot going on at work, in addition to the wedding, the remodeling and that mess with Demitri. I am always worrying about you and the baby. It is exhausting."

Mychal rubbed his shoulder to comfort him, "It's okay honey. We are fine. In a few weeks we will be married and the house will be renovated by the summer. You and Tony will figure out the problems at work and by the beginning of August we will be parents."

Richard pulled into a parking space and killed the engine. He turned to Mychal and sarcastically said, "Is it really going to be that easy?"

"Hell no!" she burst out laughing and he joined her. Once they regained themselves, Mychal added, "But it will be worth it. I promise."

Richard was grinning from ear to ear

now. He leaned over and pecked her on the lips, "That is why I love you woman, you keep me smiling. Come on so we can get this food business out of the way. I want to go baby shopping."

"Yes sir, Captain Grumpy!" she saluted.

Later that evening they skipped dinner and had a large dessert at the house, followed by her slowly massaging his body to help Richard relax. He in turn took his time carefully pleasing her before fulfilling both their needs. Afterward, she laid in his arms, back against his chest with Richard rubbing her harden abdomen. He was making senseless patterns with his index finger.

"I know what you are doing. Quit it."

Richard feigned ignorance, "I have no idea what you are talking about."

"I want him or her to settle down and go to sleep. We have jostled that child around enough for one night," she yawned.

He kissed her ear, "I was not done. I was just giving you a breather."

"Dirty old man. Quit sabotaging my efforts to sleep here," Mychal joked.

Richard's body tensed, "What did you just say?"

Puzzled, Mychal repeated, "You are sabotaging my efforts here to go to sleep."

He hugged her tight and whispered in her ear, "You are a genius!"

Still puzzled, Mychal said, "Okay, you are excited because I'm calling you out and I am a genius. And you think I am the crazy one."

He maneuvered himself to completely face her, "You are a crazy thing and you never cease to amaze me. *Mi Dios te amo.*"

Richard made love to Mychal with renewed passion. As she lay asleep his mind was already making a list of things to do on Monday at work. For once in months, he felt like the burden of work was not so insurmountable.

Richard told Mychal at the beginning of the week he would be home late almost every night. She understood because she too needed some time to close out the semester and finalize wedding plans. Thursday morning Richard asked

Mychal to go to an appointment for him with the sommelier. Sometime later she realized what the appointment was for and asked Susanna for help.

"Mychal, I do not know anything about picking wines," Susanna was doubtful.

Mychal threw up her hands, "And I do? I can't even participate in the testing."

"You can have a sip or two," her future sister-in-law teased.

Susanna had no problem finding the small wine shop on the *Plaza*. They were greeted by an ancient man who was shorter than Susanna. He only spoke Castilian which made Mychal glad she brought the younger woman. Though her Castilian Spanish was getting better, it was not well enough to conduct business. She never really practiced at home because Richard, the family and most at the university spoke English regularly. Susanna said something that made the old man laugh. She turned to Mychal and said, "I told him you were a sorry partner for this task."

Mychal rolled her eyes, "Ha ha."

"What kind of wine do you want?"

"I don't know. Something appropriate for a spring wedding I guess."

"*Algo apropiado para la primavera,*" Susanna told the older man.

The gentlemen went in the back and came out with two wines on his tray. He was followed by a much younger man with another tray. The first thing Mychal noticed was that the younger man had long sandy brown hair below his collar and kind hazel eyes. He nodded to her but tried to contain a shy smile when he saw Susanna. Both men sat trays in front of the women.

"*Este es mi aprendiz*, Javier. *Él le ayudará con el nombramiento.* He will help *por favor, para mí*," the ancient gentlemen said in broken English, surprising Mychal who had the initial thought he only spoke Castilian.

"Señoritas, *sería mi placer*," Javier did a half bow.

"My pleasure as well, I mean *tengo el placer de conocerte*," Mychal tried.

"You speak English?" Javier's words came tumbling out.

"Yes, I am American," Mychal glanced at Susanna who was seemingly dumbstruck to quiet. "My future sister-in-law does also. I guess just not right now."

Susanna blushed.

"Well then, let me explain the wines to you as we go." Javier went on to show the women he was a masterful apprentice. The four wines his supervisor chose were very good ones. The first and third were too dry for Mychal. After a tiny sip she made a face. Susanna drank two glasses and asked questions that Mychal thought were silly and slightly slurred. After all it was before noon and she was drinking wine probably on an empty stomach. Mychal had never seen this side of the younger woman, giddy, nervous, over talkative and a little ditsy. At the end of the appointment, she suggested Javier walk Susanna outside for fresh air while she attempted to handle the selections. The young man looked puzzled and explained her request to his boss.

"*Sí, sí, no hay problema,*" the old man

waved him off.

Mychal picked out a case each of the two wines she liked and was handling the bill when the pair returned. They were talking about the wedding from what she could understand. Mychal hated to break up the fun, but she was getting hungry.

"Señor . . ." she began.

"Cervantes-Baustista, but please Javier."

"Thank you for helping out. I do not think we were quite prepared for this visit. I hope Susanna was polite to you," she smiled sweetly.

"Of course Mychal. After a little air, Javier and I were just talking about your wedding and hoping for a beautiful day," Susanna blushed.

"Good, then I will expect him there," Mychal caught them both off guard. "Señor, I mean Javier, please come join us. You can supervise the delivery yourself and stay for the festivities."

"Oh, no Señorita. Señor Plasençia would not-"

"Yes he would. Please tell him what I am requesting," Mychal was a little firm.

Reluctantly, Javier conveyed her wishes to his boss.

"Also, tell him there is extra in it for you if you attend," Mychal cut in.

Javier nervously relayed that as well. Señor Plasençia broke into a broad smile and managed in broken English, "Good chance for *conexiones de negocios*."

"Great. Javier exchange phone

numbers with Susanna. She will be your point of contact over the next few weeks," Mychal smiled at her own cleverness. *"Gracias Señor* Plasençia. *Gracias Javier. Espero veros pronto."*

When Susanna got into the car, Mychal was already talking to Richard on the phone, "Yes honey, the wine appointment went great. I hope you make it home for dinner. I am making a chicken and pasta dish I got from Ruby. I love you too."

As soon as she hung up Susanna said, "You think you are so clever."

"Yep!"

After a pause she said, "He is cute."

Mychal nodded, "And interested."

The young woman blushed again,

"Very sweet and a gentleman."

"And single I hope," Mychal pulled off. "I would hate to have done all that for nothing."

"He is single."

"How do you know?"

"He told me."

Mychal chuckled, "And here I thought it was just an innocent break for some air. I am so naïve."

"You practically made him walk me outside," Susanna interjected.

"Yes, I did and you can thank me later. Now I want fast food. No Richard on this excursion means I can eat what I like. He complains I always want junk food." She shot Susanna a quick look, "We are not telling him about my invitation to Javier until he needs to know.

Susanna agreed quickly, "Oh definitely."

Richard spent the majority of the week pouring over incident reports and re-interviewing workers. He also studied the insurance photos and eyewitness report to the accidents that cost the company both money and some reputation. He was at the dock office talking to the union rep when the fire alarm went off. Panic seized Richard but he said to Tony, "We've got to get everyone out of here."

Richard worked along with his foreman, brother and the union representative to make sure everyone left the area and met on the other side of the security fence. The large crowd parted for fire and rescue workers to enter the loading area. Richard could tell the workers were uneasy. He heard their whispers but could not let them fuel his own growing suspicions. Quickly he gathered security, the foremen, Tony and the union rep to devise a counter measure. It was decided to let the day crew have the rest of the afternoon off with pay providing the authorities did not need them for questioning. The late shift would come in the last four hours of their shift if the area was secured and released by the fire department. The whole situation was going to be another financial hit, but the safety of others was at stake.

With most of the workers calm and secured, Richard thought his nightmare was over until the press showed up. Disgusted, he fielded questions until his security chief called for him saying it was urgent. Behind the barrier, Evan Barbosa told Richard there was no urgent matter, he was just saving him from the press. Richard thanked his trusted lieutenant and breathed a sigh of relief.

"Richard, the fire marshal needs to speak with you, us, and everybody. The union rep, security, everybody," Tony appeared shaken. Evan went to collect more security personnel, while Tony went to find the union rep and Richard located his foreman. Within ten minutes, a group of twenty-five converged on the firemen standing by the forklift.

The only man not dressed in gear stepped forward, "Señor Garçia-Torrés?"

Richard stepped out of the crowd, "*Sí* what happened? I was told you needed to meet with me but I hope you are okay with bringing my group of concerned leadership *Capitán . . . Sargento . . .* "

"Captain Barrentos," they shook hands. "I see you prefer English. I do not know if all your men will be able to see the problem."

"They can hear you. Please, what happened?"

The fire marshal showed Richard the front of the forklift where the metal seemed to be ripped. Then he pointed out a large pool of diesel fuel under the machine that was covered with some kind of granules that soaked up spills. "Someone smelled the fuel earlier and pulled the fire alarm as he should have, crisis averted. But sir, you have bigger problems here. See that metal in front, it was cut and twisted to drag the ground. These machines are sturdy and the metal is welded to a reinforced bumper to

114

protect the tank beneath in case of an accident. The metal on the front looks ragged because it was dragged on the ground for a period of time. Closer examination shows the edges at the top are not jagged but smoother, meaning it once was a clean cut. At the other end there are ridged, scratch tool marks and small dents in the metal like it was purposely angled downward. Every time the forklift jolted around the metal would scrape the ground creating sparks. If those sparks would have ignited the diesel fuel or even the vapors, the explosion could have taken out this whole area, materials and people."

"*Maldito infierno!*" Richard flew into a rage.

Taken back, the captain said, "Calm down, Señor Garçia-Torrés. Whoever did this was sloppy. The cut was a little too neat to be a tear and the gas line was clearly cut. The movement of the machine made the cut open wider instead of a slow leak which was the reason someone was able to see and smell all the fuel running out."

All Richard could do was shake his head speechless. His mind whirled with the possible outcomes had the scenario played out as someone had planned.

"Señor, " Captain Barrentos snapped him out of his thoughts, "we are going to need your cooperation in this case."

"Case?"

"*Sí* señor. Attempted arson is a criminal matter. With the magnitude of what could have happened, possible attempted murder charges could be introduced. We will need to take the forklift to our lab and coordinate our efforts with you for personnel to be interviewed."

"*Sí nada.* I was here today conducting my own investigation and interviews," Richard's jaw set in a grim line.

The captain looked at Richard through narrowed eyes, "What were you investigating, if I may ask?"

He gave the captain a straight look and said, "Sabotage."

5
Siblings and Security

"I am not going to summer school Richard. I am tired of school and I want a break," Susanna stood her ground in front of her brother.

He was in his study downstairs with stacks of paper on his desk. Richard was beyond stressed and not in the mood for the current discussion. He was working from home today for a few reasons. One, their new bed was being delivered that afternoon. Two, his Aston Martin coupe was at the dealership getting major bodywork. And three, he wanted to get away from his office which was slowly beginning to feel like a padded cell on the fifth floor in a hospital. Right now he did not want his frustration to show, so he calmly said, "Why do you need a break?"

"Because I want to do something different for the summer. I have been in some form of school since I was five. I have never done anything but go to school and do what is expected of me. Just this summer, I want to do what I want to do. Not what is expected of me," Susanna squared up, crossing her arms.

A tired sigh escaped Richard. Ignoring the throbbing in his head he said, "What do you want to do?"

"I want to explore life *hermano*. I need to live outside these four walls, I call a life. I need to see what is beyond Madrid, experience more night life, and meet people other than your business associates. I want to get my own identity separate from being your little sister and Tony's twin. You have to admit even Tony has changed since he started working with the family business. Instead of being the younger, cuter Garçia-Torrés brother, he is now Antonio C. Garçia-Torrés, dashing young leader climbing the corporate ladder," she gave Richard a sarcastic grin. "He has finally grown up, my brother who spent his time womanizing as Tony the *canalla* is gone. All hail the new and improved twin."

The cuter Garçia-Torrés brother Richard frowned, briefly wondering who said that. Back to the issue at hand, he knew the heart of the underlying issue was her need for independence. Without thinking, he replied, "Well, who are you trying to be?"

"I do not know because all I have ever been is the person other people wanted me to be. I was born a twin, so I started life with a prefixed identity. I was the only girl, so my identity growing up was little sister. Mama and Papa put me in music because that is what they wanted. Now I love music, but what about dance, soccer or writing? I love other things too. When they passed, you continued their wants which meant school and music. But at almost twenty-four, don't you think it is time to grow past Susanna, the musical twin who cannot do anything but live off her trust fund?" she put her hands on her hips for emphasis.

Richard knew what she was saying was true. He just could not think straight enough right now to give her his full attention. He needed Mychal to help him with this argument and at the present moment she was shopping with Ruby. "*Mañana por favor* Susanna. Can we talk about this tomorrow? Please?"

"Well, while you are thinking about things, I will not be home for my birthday this weekend," she threw in.

"What? Really Susanna, you are going overboard and testing my patience," Richard was blown away by her ending comment. He had no idea where she was going and who was she going to be with all weekend.

"What is the problem? Tony will be out all night for his birthday just like every birthday since he was eighteen. Silly me, I forgot that fact. If we share the same day, why can't we do the same thing?" his sister stated in a matter of fact tone.

Richard massaged his temples as if

the movement would make this whole situation go away. Her barb about her twin brother was not lost on him. "*Mañana hermana. Mañana.*"

Susanna tried to keep from smiling at her victory. She knew that the 'tomorrow' comment meant he needed to talk with Mychal, who was usually on her side.

"I like the dresses we picked out," Ruby was finishing her tiramisu.

"Me too," Mychal licked her spoon. "I was surprised that it was not hard to find a maternity wedding dress. Thanks for going with me. Susanna is dating and Richard is busy handling all the problems at work."

The older woman asked, "How is that going?"

Mychal sighed, "He is really stressed out. He has too much going on even with his siblings' help. He insisted the baby's room and his office be completed before my mother gets here. Something about showing her the baby will have a place to sleep. I think the real issue is meeting my family."

"You think so? That does not sound like Richard."

"I am only guessing that his motivation is to impress my mother. He does not truly know her beyond the few occasions they talked on the phone and what he learned from all my stories. We video chatted a few times with him in the background, but face to face is a different matter. I think it reminds him of how much he misses his own parents," Mychal felt the baby move. "Easy little one. Didn't you like dessert?"

Ruby chuckled, "Do you still not want to know the sex of the baby?"

"Nope, but I secretly have my favorite of all the names. Rohas if it is a boy and Alejandra if it is a girl," Mychal smiled.

"Let me guess, his parents' names."

Mychal continued to smile.

"Why not your parents' names?"

Her smile wavered a little, "My mother's name is Tia and to be honest, I never really knew mine and Max's father. They were married but never really together. My mom was with Riley and Reese's dad most of my life. When I was nine and Max was eleven, our father died in a truck driving accident in his native home of St. Maarten. My mom waited another ten years to marry their dad, her second husband."

Ruby seemed whimsical, "I always assumed you grew up in a classic American family with a mom, dad, dog and white picket fence."

"Far from it. We grew up in the Bronx in a multifamily home. My grandparents lived upstairs and we were downstairs. My mom got a small dog after we left home and no white picket fence. I can't complain about how I grew up because my life was not that bad. However, the situation was enough to give me motivation to achieve my dreams," Mychal looked down in her empty plate.

Ruby patted her hand, "That's right; when life gives you limes you make margaritas. So when is your mother coming?"

"Next Monday."

"Summer school classes are just starting. Your courses will have been in less than a month, your family is coming, and you are finishing the plans for a wedding. *Mi Dios! Estás demente!*"

"I know. She and my sister will be here for a week and my brother will be here less than a week. We are postponing the honeymoon until after they leave," Mychal signaled for the bill.

"Where are you two going?"

"On our Thailand trip I think. I wanted to go somewhere closer, that way we could save our tropical destination for later, but Richard insisted we go now before the baby comes. There will be no more romantic vacations for two after that. After we consulted the doctor for travel safety approval, I was not going to argue and add more stress on top of work problems still bothering him."

"Still problems with possible sabotage?" the older woman asked.

"Yes. Last week a deliberate act to blow up a forklift shut the dock down for hours. When Richard got home he was exhausted. He hired more security and now the authorities are involved," Mychal could not keep the sourness out of her voice.

Ruby shook her head, "The timing of those incidents is so horrible. The poor man."

"I know, he is so overwhelmed. That is why I have tried to make this a simple wedding, but it turned into a huge family slash business affair. Everything is set. My sister and mother will get my mom's dress Tuesday. We will pick out dresses for my three bridesmaids today and still have time for alterations," Mychal gathered her bag.

"Luis and I are like teenagers. It has been ages since we were in a wedding party," Ruby smiled.

"It was Richard's idea. He even telephoned my older brother to ask for my hand in marriage." Mychal grinned at the memory. "I thought of asking Max to escort me, then changed my mind. So my brother will escort our mother and then stand with Tony and Luis."

"I'm glad your family can come to support you."

"Me too. Only one of my brothers and my sister are able to come though. With all that has happened at home, my in-laws and nieces could not come. My other brother could not make it due to finances. I guess it is for the best that way," she shrugged.

"How are things going with that situation? Besides making life uneasy between you and your sister," Ruby asked.

"Max really wanted to stay out of it at first, now he is considering hiring an accountant to work through the mess. It needs to be determined what funds were used for different investments. Just how much was my money and how much was the government's money that Jake used. A slow process according to Max." Changing subjects she said, "My office was moved Thursday."

"To where? We are struggling for space in the department."

"The office beside Stephan Ferrara. The storage space will be my old office. The old classroom they were using for storage will be the new graduate assistants' office and I will be in their old space."

"Oh," Ruby rubbed her hands together, "more space in the old classroom means more graduate students."

"I hope so. This summer I am teaching the thesis seminar and an online hybrid research class. Just in case I do not make it to the end of summer session," Mychal rubbed her junior soccer ball sized abdomen.

"You will make it. Babies come in their own time."

"I know. Secretly, I think we will

make great parents," Mychal grinned.

Ruby gave her a motherly hug, "I know you will be great parents."

"Susanna is being defiant again," Richard said after kissing Mychal hello.

"Hello to you too."

Richard plopped back in his chair, "She is refusing to go to summer school and she is spending the weekend, her birthday weekend, away from the family."

Mychal made a face, "And?"

"And? *Bella* that is unacceptable," he shook his head.

"Why?" she did not understand.

"What do you mean why? Whose side are you on?"

Mychal was still in the dark, "I still don't understand. She wants to spend the weekend with friends her own age. Then she wants to sit out the summer semester, giving her the whole summer off. Did she say she was joining a traveling circus of clowns or something during this time?"

"No, she said that she does not want to do anything. She said she wants to find herself. She said she is tired of being the little twin sister."

"Oh, I see. She wants to spread her proverbial wings or test the waters," Mychal paused before making a point, "like Tony is doing now by joining the company."

Silence enveloped the room.

Richard made a sour face, "These are the moments I love you, but your usual blunt honesty can go to hell."

Mychal said nothing, hoping he would come to his senses.

"So what do you want me to do? Let her run wild in the streets to become *un payaso loco*?"

She sighed and finally said, "In three months or so we will have our own child to parent. Boy or girl, they will need your full capacity to be their dad. I know you stepped up and became the family patriarch when your parents passed. That being said, that was a temporary situation. Your siblings are just that, siblings. Ones that you have done your best in guiding them to adulthood. But, honey, they are adults that are trying to live their lives if you would just ease up. Don't you think it is time you lived yours?"

Richard said nothing while staring out the window. Mychal came to sit across his lap and hugged him. He hugged her back, burying his face in the hollow of her neck. They sat that way for a while, neither speaking. He finally said, "It is hard to let go. I feel like I am losing control. The company has problems, my household is in chaos and on top of all of this, I feel like I cannot even protect you and my unborn child."

"Oh honey," she cupped his face, "you have the weight of the world on your shoulders. The household is disjointed because it is being remodeled, a short term thing. The company is recovering because you hired extra security and the police are involved. You can stop worrying about protecting me, I'm fine. But as far as Tony and Susanna, they need you to be less of a father figure and more of an adult brother for them."

Richard kissed her gently before saying, "I will try."

"That is all you can do and you can start by understanding this is her birthday weekend. Don't make a big deal about her wanting to spend it with friends. Let them both enjoy their birthday," Mychal smiled back at him. "Now change clothes. We are going out. You need a break."

"Mychal, I really cannot leave. I-"

She cut him off, "You can and you will. We are going to a jazz and poetry night. Some of the graduate students in the English and foreign language departments are sponsoring a poetry competition for undergraduate students. The university's jazz music students are providing intercession music between competition rounds. Come on, it will be fun."

He tried to put up a feeble argument but she was not entertaining what Richard had to say. When he left, Mychal sat in his office looking at the once neat space now filled with piles of paper and photos. His computer was on and opened to an email. She was about to look away until the word university caught her eye. She briefly glanced over the email only to see that his security chief had assigned someone to support the campus security officers that would check on Mychal's whereabouts and building daily when the semester started. Why would Richard do that and not even tell her? Before she could speculate, Mychal heard Richard's footsteps across the kitchen floor. She quickly got up to meet him at the door with a hungry kiss to distract him.

Mychal's kisses always ignited Richard's desire. He broke their kiss and said, "*Bella*, if you kiss me like that again, we will not make it to your students' event."

"I just wanted to let you know I love you."

"And you know I love you. Let me close down my office and we are gone." He gave no notice to whether his email had been read.

Despite his worries Richard enjoyed the evening. He was impressed with the poetry and loved the music. He frequently squeezed Mychal's hand and kissed her. On the way home he talked about work and the security that was now in place. Mychal could see he was more relaxed than he had been in a while. When they arrived at the house, she coaxed him into a midnight swim. Frolicking in the water like teenagers, they talked about her anxieties with her family coming to visit.

"I thought you would be happy your family was coming for the wedding," Richard floated on his back beside Mychal.

"I am, sort of. There was always some tension between my sister and I growing up. Now we have grown distant since this whole thing with her husband happened. When Jacob went to jail, she lost the major household income provider. Their loss was so substantial, that they moved into my mother's house. I moved my mom into my home when I left so she could rent hers out for the extra income. That idea is useless now because my mom insisted Riley needed a place to stay." Thinking about this conversation, all she could do was shake her head.

"I know you told me they moved into your mother's house. I had no idea your mom just let them move in with no responsibilities."

"Yep, same stuff on a different day. Same selfish ass Riley. She would have taken advantage of everything else I left for mom if my mother had her way. Max put a stop to that. Nothing has changed. When we were kids mom bailed Riley out of everything. She would say Max and Mychal are going to be fine but it was Riley and Reece that kept her worried all the time," Mychal looked at the water as if the memories were playing on some invisible screen.

"*Hola Bella,*" Richard stood beside her, "*volver del viejo malos recuerdos.*"

She looked at him and smiled, "*Estoy aquí. Yo nunca dejaré de usted. Nunca.*"

He broke into a broad grin, "Someone has been working on their *Castilian*."

"*Sí*," she moved back into the shallow end of the pool then threw her bikini top at him.

"*Bella*, what are you doing?"

"Come find out," came her response along with her bikini bottom.

Richard swam underwater to her. She could feel his lips on her abdomen before he surfaced to kiss her mouth. He moved to her ear and whispered, "You are such a temptress."

Her response was to work off his swim trunks and brush against his evident desire. Richard swore loudly as he suckled her earlobe. Weightless and graceful thanks to the water, she eased on him and wrapped her legs around his hips. He let out a long sigh. Richard walked them an arm's length from the wall. He braced them with one hand and moved her hips with the other. The water made the whole movement a slow dance.

"Dar a mí," Richard had both hands on her hips urging their pace. Mychal claimed his mouth as her thighs tightened around his hips. Her spasms were absorbed by their watery surroundings. Her multiple spasms triggered his own body's response. Richard wrapped his arms around her body and trembled while whispering something in Spanish against her neck. All Mychal could make out was 'love you' and 'my world'. They stayed embraced for a long moment, neither wanting to move.

Finally he said, "You planned this whole evening knowing I needed a little something different, a break. Thank you love."

"Oh sir, it was my pleasure," she moved to uncouple them. "I know you are exhausted from the extra problems at work. I hear it when you talk in your sleep. You never did that before."

"Sorry, I did not realize that was happening," Richard blushed with embarrassment.

"Don't be sorry honey. I know you think that the baby and me are in danger. We are not. I know you hired extra security to keep tabs on me on campus, but I am fine. I really do not want someone following me, but if it puts your mind at ease, I will play nice," Mychal smirked.

Richard gave her a weak guilty smile, "Do not be upset *Bella*. I am only trying to protect you. I handpicked Iroh. He trained in several martial arts including krav maga. He has high marksman scores and is a master of incognito."

Mychal had to admit she was impressed. Maybe after the baby and this mess was over, she could train with him. Richard interrupted her thoughts, "He has offered to train you with a gun."

"No!" shot out on reflex. Realizing she might alarm Richard, she said, "I do not like guns. Period. But if it makes you feel better, I will carry a weapon of my choosing."

"I can only guess what kind of ninja toys you can possibly have. But it will make me feel better. Even though I am not sure what you could carry in your condition," he frowned.

"Don't worry. I have been trained in a dozen weapons. I will pick one."

Richard smiled easy thinking 'that's my girl' but said, "Good. Extra security will be here Monday. In addition to what we have now, there will be dogs. We will receive training on how to handle the dogs on Monday and Tuesday."

"What about my mom and sister?"

"They will receive the training words as well. As long as they are here, they are under my protection."

A thought occurred to Mychal, "Did the current security see us skinny dipping?"

"Um maybe. I hope they enjoyed the show, I know I did," he started walking toward the step, gracefully guiding her. Richard got out of the water to get their towels. She admired his dimpled buttocks as he walked. He made no move to hand one to her.

"Towel?"

"You want a towel? What did you say before? 'Come find out' I think it was," Richard joked.

"Fine," Mychal slowly exited the pool knowing Richard was watching her wet curvy body in the moonlight.

He handed her a towel and said, "Absolutely beautiful."

"Glad you liked the view. Me and the baby are hungry. You want something?"

"Maybe a sandwich. And wine. Go on in and I will be right behind you. I need to fish out our swimwear so it does not clog the filters."

Richard retrieved the pool net from its place beside the pool house. He collected their clothing and returned the net to its place. A noise caught his attention. It almost sounded like a sob. Blaming fatigue and worry, he ignored it. But even as Richard made his way to the house, he developed a creepy feeling he was being watched.

6
Family and Nuptials

Against Mychal's wishes, Iroh, her personal security went with her to the airport. She tried to argue with Richard before leaving, but he would not be swayed. After a few minutes of discussion, he swore loudly and barked, "This is not up for debate! Iroh will take you to the airport and that is final!"

Knowing not to press him, Mychal conceded to let herself be driven to the airport. She did not mind her personal protection, he was actually quite likeable.

Iroh was an average size man of mixed Asian heritage that wore regular clothes and surfer shades. Richard was right about him just blending in because he looked like one of her students. Mychal liked him immediately despite his given duty. They had a lengthy conversation about martial arts and weapons on the morning they were introduced. Now thirty-six hours later, he was her shadow, which included being her chauffeur.

"You will tell my mother you are my assistant that Richard has hired to help me with the wedding. She will know nothing about what you do. I will text you when we go out and where we are going. Remember we cannot set them off to what is going on."

He looked at the road, "*Sí* Señorita."

"Again with the Señorita. What did

we agree on?" she teased.

"*Sí* Doc," he smiled.

Once inside the airport Mychal's stomach was in knots waiting for her family. She was not sure if it was the baby or nerves. She texted her sister to let them know she was at the information hub.

"You okay doctor?" Iroh appeared out of nowhere, making her jump.

Richard was right; he was the master of inconspicuous.

"I thought you were waiting in the car."

"I cannot protect you from the car," he dryly retorted.

Impulsively, Mychal asked, "Iroh, are you protecting me from a situation or a person?"

"My God, Mychal Scott Ayscue! Look at you!" a raspy voice with a deep New York accent interrupted them. "Riley! Riley! Get over here. I found ya sista and she swallowed a basketball!"

Her bodyguard shot her a disbelieving look as her mother walked over and squeezed Mychal hard enough to wind her. She hugged back, laughing. Her mother never changed. At five and a half feet she was three inches shorter than her daughter and was the picture of a typical East Bronx Italian New Yorker. Tia had an olive complexion like half of her children with dyed jet black hair. As usual, she wore heavy makeup with bright red lips. She was wearing jeans too young for her age and a black NYFD t-shirt.

"Ma, it's good to see you."

"And you darling," she kissed both

Mychal's cheeks. "Where is Richard and who is this?"

"Ma this is Iroh. He's a . . . he's my assistant that Richard hired to help me with the wedding," Mychal almost forgot her own lie.

"Assistant? How fancy," Tia looked around, "Where is ya sista? Riley!"

"Ma, stop hollering, I am right here," Mychal's sister came up behind them looking like a younger version of their mother, makeup and all. She took one look at Mychal and said, "Knocked up uh? Of all the things to do in Spain, this is what you picked? Why couldn't you be like other tourists and just steal the towels from a fancy hotel?"

"Funny," Mychal hugged her sister and whispered in her ear, "Why is your mother so loud?"

"Imagine the plane ride with her. There was not enough liquor on that plane for me or her," Riley shook her head.

Mychal chuckled, "That bad?"

"Horrible," her sister exclaimed, rolling her eyes. "Who is this?"

"That is Mychal's personal assistant for the wedding," their mom interjected. "He appears to be a nice man, so don't get no funny ideas. *Capeesh*?"

"Ma!" Mychal exclaimed at the same time Riley declared, "Oh God!"

Mychal shot Iroh a sympathetic look to which he responded with a sly grin. After collecting their luggage and the Range Rover, Mychal settled in for the long ride. Sure enough her mother asked questions all the way to the house. Her sister sat in the back with Mychal making small talk about the wedding. Mychal must have closed her eyes for a moment because her mother's loud exclamation startled her. "Oh my God! This place is so beautiful!"

She smiled at her mother's reaction and how similar it was to her own when she first turned down the driveway and saw the flowers on the property.

"Wow sis, you really hooked a rich one," her sister commented looking out the window. "Personal assistant, fancy cars and a mansion; no wonder you got pregnant."

Mychal knew it was coming out at some point, just not this early – the ever jealous Riley. She felt her temper creeping over her mental horizon, but she said, "It's not like that. I did not plan any of this."

"Sure you didn't sis," Riley mumbled to Mychal but looked out the window as they approached the house. Mychal mentally counted to thirty-seven before she was calm again. She needed Richard near to settle her nerves. She was almost sure they would embarrass her once in the house.

Mychal was not a psychic, but she was right on target about her mother. Upon walking in the house they both were impressed, except her mother was loud and crass, while her sister was sullen and pouty. She showed them the main areas, the living room, and the kitchen with the adjourning family room, before taking them upstairs to their rooms. She put her mother in the nursery which was across the hall and her sister in the small guest room across from Susanna's room at the end of the hall.

Mychal really wished the

renovations on the back wing apartment were done. She even suggested that Richard put them up in a hotel. His response was he could not protect them in a hotel and that they needed to be at the house for the dog training. They would all be cramped upstairs for a week. Oh joy. She went downstairs for a snack for the baby's sake and her own piece of mind.

As she sat at the kitchen island eating pita chips with hummus, her sister came in. Mychal sighed and prepared herself for battle. "Where's Ma?"

"Upstairs. She was unpacking but is probably going through your personal things by now," her sister sat across from her on another bar stool at the island. "So how do you like being pregnant?"

"It's okay, I guess. I eat a lot, sleep like a stone and worry," Mychal regretted that last word as soon as she said it.

"What are you worried about? This is the life," her sister was shocked.

"There's a bunch of stuff going on at Richard's company. He thinks something will happen at the wedding. He thinks somebody is trying to hurt me. He is worried, so I am worried about his stress level."

"Who is trying to hurt my sister? And why did you keep that from me?" Riley was getting upset.

"Calm down and watch your voice Riley. I am fine. I don't need you to turn into Stewey Bricks from the neighborhood," Mychal shot her sister a grimace.

Riley burst out laughing, "He ain't Stewey Bricks any more, he is Michael Steward, celebrity personal trainer and math teacher at Nassau Community College."

At that Mychal too lost her composure to laughter, "He was such a small kid. Nobody knew how strong he was from carrying around bricks."

"He knew the value of family then and boy if you messed with his brothers and sisters, it was going down in the street," her sister chimed in.

"Wonder where he kept getting those bricks from?" Mychal looked puzzled, then laughed again.

Taking a deep breath, Riley said, "It's good to laugh. There have been too many tears."

Mychal did not respond and kept looking out the window at the pool.

Quietly, her sister said, "I know it's not entirely your fault. Jacob's not a bad guy."

Mychal could not believe her ears. It almost sounded like her sister was trying to misplace some blame. She whipped around, amber eyes blazing with anger, "Not entirely my fault? Is that what you believe? I was trying to help him start his business. I believed in him just like you did. When Jacob told me he got government grants to keep the business afloat, I was happy for him. Then I noticed less money was for the business and more went to your household. After your trip to the Mediterranean, I knew something was wrong. Nobody takes a trip like that and comes home to buy a new Mercedes and a boat. I confronted his lying ass, or don't you remember that argument? I told him I wanted to cash out and he called you

159

saying I was being unreasonable and trying to hurt the business."

"Come on sis, he was and still is my husband. I had to take-"

"And I was and still am your sister Riley! Someone who worked hard for everything I had," Mychal snapped back.

"Oh here we go again with the Ma always treated us different story. The Ma gave you the world and I had to work for everything story. When are you going to get over that?" her sister rolled her eyes.

"When you admit it is true," Mychal hissed. "Max and I worked for every little thing from her attention to building our careers. I worked my ass off in school, worked harder at the dojo for my black belt and poured my all into my career. I was fortunate to get that job at the university and even luckier to get my book published. For all my efforts, I was not going to let your husband drag me down with him."

"So, was that the real problem? That I got married before you and we had more than you? All you had was your precious black belt and career."

Richard heard loud voices as soon as he walked into the house from the garage. He quickened to the kitchen but stopped when he heard Mychal say, "None of what you had was a problem for me and I was never jealous of you or your marriage. If you really thought that, then you would have said something when I stepped in to help your husband start his business. But you had no clue how he got all that money to keep the business and your lifestyle afloat until after that nasty argument he and I had at Christmas. All you cared about was the stuff you got from being Mrs.

Jacob Adams. You wanted to show me, Max and everyone else in the neighborhood that Riley Delarenzo, former cheerleader and community college alumni, was just as good as or better than everyone else."

"Good one sis. Oh, please do not let me and everyone else ever forget we have two doctors in the family," Riley sneered.

"It is not about that and it never was! I wanted out of your husband's business. Period, point blank. It took a turn in a direction that I just could not support. You took it personal because you thought it was an attempt to make his business fail and you look bad. Again, like I said, the reason for that last argument was the business books looked suspect to me, a layman with no real business sense. So I took my money and left to protect me and my investments. Whatever happened after I left was not my fault. If you would see me as an investor

162

and not some type of know-it-all sister out to make you look like a fool, maybe you would understand."

"But you did not end up in jail. You are not even under investigation," her sister's anger appeared to have lost some steam.

"No, I did not go to jail. Will that make you happy? Do you want me to have an arrest record to match my other notable accomplishments?"

"Mychal. I did not mean it like that."

Mychal was in disbelief that her sister even thought her being in equal trouble would somehow amend the situation. "Well what did you mean? You want me to be in the same trouble that Jake is in too? Well I am under some kind of investigation. Max is working on it sorting everything out. Didn't Ma tell you?"

"Are you kidding? All she talks about is your wedding and the baby. If it ain't how she can die happy now that her last child is married off, she doesn't talk about anything else. So no."

"She never told you about the visit from state department agents. Even Richard got a call."

Riley shook her head, "Nothing. Mostly everybody has been trying to help us get stabilized after everything was seized and frozen."

"I know. Max told me," Mychal choked back her emotions.

Softly and humbly, her sister said, "Thanks for helping us out sis. I know you didn't have to, especially after all that has happened. I would not have blamed you if you said no to letting Ma continue to stay in your house so we could move into hers."

"You are still my sister Riley. I would not see you homeless and I know moving in with Ma at my place would be an additional punishment," Mychal shook her head.

"You don't know the half of it. If I hear one more 'I told you so' and how Jacob is a jerk, I'm going to lose it. He is still my husband," Riley sighed.

Mychal sighed too.

"*Bella*," Richard took the chance to come in the room, "I see our family has arrived."

He hugged and kissed her then turned to Riley, who was a shorter curvier version of his fiancée with enough makeup on to look like war paint given the situation he just heard, "You must be my new sister-in-law."

"Hello handsome! Looks like my sister finally got a prince," she stuck out her hand.

"We do not do that with family," Richard grabbed and hugged her. "I am glad you could make it Riley."

"Me too Richard."

"Mychal, see what everyone wants for dinner and call in the order. Ask Iroh if he will pick it up from the restaurant. The dog trainer starts this evening. He is bringing a set of dogs tonight and if needed a set tomorrow night. We will all be training on various commands over the next forty-eight hours."

"Why do we need to be involved in that? Is it part of the wedding? Mychal never said you were a dog lover, even though I know she is," Riley inquired.

Mychal held her breath. They had not discussed what they would actually say if there were any questions about the security. Richard noticed her body language and took her hand, squeezing it as if to say 'I got this'.

"For some years I dated a minor celebrity and had my picture in *el tabloide local*. I want to spare my bride any extra media attention. This should be her day. So I hired security including dogs to make sure that happens."

"Rich and famous, you go sis," her sister teased.

"You are too kind Riley. *Bella*, please collect orders while I take a shower. You know what I want from wherever you order," he kissed her and left.

Riley waited until he was gone to say, "You better not tell Ma about that!"

"You either!"

The sisters chorused their laughter. Their girlish humor seemed to deflate the rest of the tension from their earlier squabble. Her sister said, "I like him for you. It's obvious he loves you."

"Yeah and I him. He is a perfect gentleman unless he is stressed or hungry. Get Ma while I text Tony and Susanna so we can order. He means business when it comes to food."

Mychal placed the orders for seven people from one of Richard's favorite restaurants. During dinner, their mother quizzed him and his siblings like a talk show host. Mychal and Riley were overly embarrassed, which amused Richard, Susanna and Tony. The three were very accommodating to her mother which was met with eye rolling and heavy sighs. She and her sister took turns attempting to censure their mother by exclaiming, "Ma please" when her questioning went too far.

After dinner, the dog trainer arrived with four large carriers. The trainer's assistant took each dog out and allowed it to walk around while they waited for Tony to change and Susanna to run a quick errand. Iroh was already there because he had picked up dinner and Pedro came shortly after the trainer. By the time Richard's siblings joined the group, the number was nine including his head of security, Evan. The group went through the dog commands which were in Dutch. The trainer made sure everyone could pronounce the commands as well as understand what each command was asking the dog to do. He spent extra time with the group due to the various accents. He really concentrated with Mychal's sister and mother because of their Yankee accents.

After their break, the trainer split them into two teams, taking turns directing the dogs in various commands. Mychal noticed one dog stayed in his kennel watching. She asked the assistant about him.

"Madam," he said in the Queen's English, "he's been a bit rambunctious."

"Well everyone has an off day. Can we try him?"

"Madam, I don't know."

"Please?" She tried again, "how about a leash?"

"This is against the company's policy, but it is getting late and we must move on," he called the dog out and hooked the leash.

"Let me," Mychal insisted. She took the leash and commanded the dog to walk. Together they trotted up to the front of the tree lined drive and back. When she took a sip of her water bottle the dog whined. Mychal bent down and let him have the rest of the bottle. Afterward the dog licked her hand then her face before heeling at her side without a command. She sat in the grass beside him rubbing the dog's head as they watched the others. The small German Shepard whined then laid on his stomach to put his head on her leg.

"Mychal," Richard called, "what are you doing? Bring that dog and come finish the training."

She groaned inward but complied. Boy, he morphed into a grouch when the dog trainer came. Secretly she earned for the wedding to be over. Mychal frowned as she walked over to him, "We were just taking a break."

"We?"

"Yeah, Solomon needed water and I needed to stretch."

Richard said nothing. He was focused on the attack portion of the training. One by one the dogs attacked the arm of the foam clad assistant. After Solomon's turn, he trotted back over to Mychal instead of Iroh who issued the command. As the sun went down, the session was drawing to a close. The assistant put away the dogs as the trainer assigned homework. When Solomon was called he looked at Mychal as if to say 'do I have to'.

"Yes you do," she answered as if the dog actually spoke. She gave the command for home and he walked into his kennel.

The assistant shook his head, "I've never seen him act like that, attached like he has been with you since a pup."

"He is a good dog. Can he stay?"

"No madam. We've got to settle them down for the night."

"Too bad. Wait." Mychal took off her Outer Banks sweatshirt. "This is for Solomon so he won't be alone tonight."

Despite the other man's objections, she bent, gave the dog a good rub and put her sweatshirt in the kennel. The dog licked her hand and laid his head on the material.

The assistant just shook his head.

As the family headed back to the house, Mychal and Susanna discussed Richard's sour mood. Susanna said, "Yeah, he is being unbearable again. He snapped at me for being late for the training. I was just next door delivering Rafael's invitation. I have not seen him since Christmas, so we were catching up. Rafael was telling me that he met someone when his uncle walked in. I had no idea anyone else was even in the house. Nice looking older gentlemen and very stately, though he had a weird Asian Spanish name. Said his name was Armand, no Amato Dellosanto and he was Rafael's mother's brother. When she passed about three years ago, I don't know if I met that uncle then at the funeral."

"I remember him from the university gala. Quite an attractive older man. He looked more like a judge or senator. He told me that Rafael's mother was not from this area. That name sounds, Asian or Middle eastern, but he said he was from Athens" Mychal shrugged.

"I didn't know any of that information. You found all that out in one night? All I knew was that she was very pretty even in her illness. They have been our neighbors since forever. Anyway, his uncle asked like a dozen questions about the area. Stuff like the economy, housing, political views, travel and trade," Susanna huffed. "It felt like I was in an interview. I didn't know what to tell him. I suggested he talk with Richard for all that information. But it would have to be any time after Saturday."

"That was nice of you," Mychal remarked.

"It was the neighborly thing to do. I'm sure Rafael did not know the answers to any of those questions. In school he was a bit clueless and always chasing women. Young or old, he had a revolving door of women at his house. I cannot wait to meet this person Rafael will be bringing to the wedding. He seemed really excited about their relationship."

"Speaking of relationships, how is yours doing? Miss taking the summer off to explore the world," she teased.

"In all honesty, there is something about Javier that is different than any other guy I have dated. He is a great person and all gentlemen. You have a good eye for picking the right guy," Susanna smiled.

"Mychal, darling hurry up and get in the house," her mother called. "Spending long hours in this night air with these dogs

176

is not good for a pregnant woman."

Mychal and Susanna exchanged baffled expressions. She spoke first, "I swear if I was not pregnant I would be drinking right now. I cannot wait for my brother to join this family circus."

The younger woman jokingly replied, "Your mother is something special."

Mychal could only say, "You have no idea. Special was a kind word, thanks for that one."

The next evening training resumed, keeping the same set of dogs because they did so well the previous night. When Solomon saw Mychal, he yipped in his kennel.

The assistant said, "Madam, I think you have made some impression on this dog."

Once out, Mychal walked Solomon around the grounds before going back to training. During their break she eased over to Richard and kissed him.

"*Bella*, what was that for?" he smiled.

"I love you and want to show you something. Stay here."

Puzzled Richard did as he was told. Minutes later heard her say '*Vind papa*' before Solomon ran around the corner and barked twice as he sat at Richard's feet. Mychal appeared grinning and gave the dog a treat. "Good boy. Now you tell him to find me. Tell him to 'find Bella'."

She disappeared before he could protest. The dog looked at him waiting. Richard sighed, "*Vind Bella*."

Solomon took off and barked twice around the corner. Both walked around the hedge happy. "Can he be my wedding present? Please? I never had a dog growing up."

He could only chuckle and say he would think about it.

In the end, Mychal almost got what she wanted. Richard agreed to see how the dog adjusted to the family. If things went well he could stay on after the assignment was over. Mychal talked the dog into the house by agreeing to be responsible for his nightly needs because the training company attended to them during the day.

That night she was nervous and wanted to make sure Solomon was adjusting. She sat at the kitchen island feeding the dog bits of the ice cream and graham crackers sundae she made when his ears perked and his body stiffened. The dog walked closer to her and issued a low growl. When the dog heard Susanna issue the command to 'heel' then followed with the 'friend' command, he went back to his graham crackers and ice cream. Mychal said to her soon to be sister-in-law, "You're out late. Anything I should know?"

Susanna sat adjacent to Mychal, smiling.

"Let me guess, Javier the wine dude? Again."

"Mychal, he is so amazingly terrific," Susanna gushed. "He is quiet, earnest and humble. He loves wines, music and dancing. We go to cafés on his lunch break and anywhere when we get time together at night. He's just right for me, not some stuck up social climber. He wants to go to a culinary school so he can design recipes to go with wines."

"Sounds like you have fallen for him. Was that before or after last weekend?" Mychal joked.

The younger woman blushed, "I know it has not been long, but he has potential to be the one."

That comment took Mychal by surprise so much she coughed on her water. She eyed Susanna like she suddenly grew a second head, "Well that is news I am sure you have not shared with your brothers."

"Tony, yes. Richard, no. Tony has even been out with us," Susanna shrugged, "You should know the reasons why I have not told Richard. He is already grouchy and stressed out. I was planning to tell him after the wedding."

"Thank you from both of us. My

future husband does not know it, but he cannot handle everybody's business."

Richard's sister laughed.

Mychal yawned, "Well I want to hear all about him over breakfast. Now that my new friend and my child have been fed, I need some sleep. Till the morning my dear."

The women bade each other goodnight at the top of the stairs. As she eased in the bed, Richard stirred enough to ask was everything okay. Mychal replied she was just checking on the dog. His response was not to get any ideas about that dog being in his wedding before rolling over and returning to sleep.

7
Weddings and Warnings

Mychal's excitement and anxiety were through the roof leading up to the wedding. When her brother Max finally flew in, it seemed to put her mind at ease. Mychal really missed him and he was emotional at the site of his pregnant sister. She insisted Iroh take the longest way home so she could spend time with her brother alone.

On the ride he updated her on how things were going in Jacob's investigation. Max discussed the alternatives as they might apply to her in the situation. Mychal listened but replied that ultimately the decisions for anything from this point forward would be made by both she and Richard. When they arrived at the house their mother gushed over having three of her children together for such a happy occasion. Their brother was on a family vacation visiting his wife's family and could not afford to fly in for the wedding. They would video chat him in for the ceremony. Richard called and invited them out to a restaurant close to his office for dinner.

During dinner he and Max really hit it off over tapas and cocktails. Mychal's older brother favored the rest of the family with the exceptions of his barrel brown hair and his height which was well over six feet. While the two oldest of Tia Delarenzo's children got height and cashew complexion from their father, her younger two got height from her. By the end of the evening, Mychal drove them home while her mom and sister rode with the ever present Iroh. She left Max and Richard up talking all night.

In the morning she woke to a note saying Richard and her brother were going out for breakfast and would bring back food for everyone else. Breakfast was a loud event with even Tony and Susanna joining. The afternoon was spent by the pool with Susanna and Richard leaving to meet with the contractor in the once closed mother-in-law wing that was now a renovated apartment. So far the structural repairs and the electrical updating was done. The drywall, painting, refinishing the floors and extras Tony and Susanna wanted were to be finalized today. As she was thinking, Max sat beside her on

Richard's chair.

"That is some guy you got there," her brother's deep bass broke her thoughts.

"Don't I know," she blushed.

"All he talked about was how happy you made him," Max chuckled, "then he told me the story about how he thought the person he hired was me when your name was on the application."

"Yeah, we had that talk on my first night. Thank God Richard got over it. I never thought I would be marrying him one day," she smiled.

"He is really nervous about this wedding. His ex-girlfriend sounds like a total whack job. All this security and dog patrols, he is not taking any chances," Max frowned. "I knew I could not get what you ordered through customs. I had it shipped instead. I hope you never need it."

"I hope so too. Believe me, I know Richard is tense. I just wonder when we get married will this whatever with her finally be over. I am really not worried about her but Richard is almost paranoid about what she might do to us. I think he is just under pressure because he is doing too much. Tony and Susanna have been a tremendous help. They really took some of the responsibility off of his always full plate. And Iroh. He keeps me and the baby safe," she rubbed her now regulation soccer ball sized abdomen. The baby moved as if in response to her touch.

"Don't you think about anything other than being healthy and saying 'I do'. Richard will handle things here and I will handle things at home," her brother held her hand.

"Thanks, I love you," Mychal squeezed his hand.

"I love you too. Now what time is this wedding party dinner?"

"Seven, but we will party after that," she winked.

"Party? You mean a bachelor party? With my sisters?"

Mychal laughed, "No! We will take in the city festivals and bars."

"Just checking. Things might be a little different in this country but a bachelor party with all my female relatives would be weird," he left to get a beer.

As they got dressed Mychal's

excitement was almost at the giddy point. She was playful while getting ready which infected Richard. She put him in a good mood. They took two separate vehicles to the restaurant where they met Ruby and Luis. The couple immediately loved Mychal's family, even though Riley seemed distracted. Mychal chose to ignore her because this was her time and her sister's attitude was not going to ruin it. On a trip to the bathroom, Mychal spotted her shadow and gave him a nod. Iroh winked but gave no other acknowledgement.

After dinner the party went for *sobremesa*. Richard was the super guy that Mychal fell in love with. He was playfully romantic all night. The entire wedding party danced and ate past midnight. Too excited with anticipation when they all got home, Mychal and Richard sat up for hours talking.

It was after one in the afternoon when the event planner arrived with the rental company. Security alerted Richard when everyone's identification and vans were checked. During a super quick lunch of pasta and fresh fruit, Ruby and Luis arrived. Next, the stylist and his crew arrived slightly flustered by the security checkpoint. They set up in the music room with three stations, hair, nails and makeup. Mychal let her mother and Ruby start while she, Riley and Susanna sat watching the flurry of activity. She turned to Susanna who was checking her phone and joked, "He is here, right?"

The younger woman's face lit up from both joy and embarrassment.

"Who?" Riley asked.

"Javier Cervantes-Baustista, the new apple in Susanna's eye," Mychal teased.

"Girl, have you been holding out on the group?" Riley joined in, "What's wrong with him? Cauliflower ears? Bad teeth? Wait, I know, he's shorter than you."

Susanna blushed crimson and Mychal burst into laughter. "Nothing is wrong with him. He is just a plain, normal guy."

"Plain?" Riley made a face. "What does that mean? No personality?"

Mychal noticed Susanna was slower to answer and said to her sister, "Like I said, nothing is wrong with him. He is actually super cute, hardworking and daring as hell."

Susanna visibly relaxed and broke into a wide grin when Riley said, "What? What? Is my sister about to have another brother-in-law?"

Finally, the younger grinning woman said, "Maybe."

Mychal helped her mother with her dress while Ruby sat under the dryer a few minutes more. Her mother was wiping tears as Mychal zipped her up.

"Ma, come on. None of that."

"I'm trying baby. I love you and I'm just so proud of you." Her mother suddenly hugged her extra tight, catching Mychal off guard, "I don't say it enough, I want your happiness and I believe you found it."

Mychal hugged back, "Me too Ma."

They were still wiping tears when Ruby came in, "Hey, what did I miss?"

"Nothing, Ma was just being all emotional today."

Ruby smiled, "It is a great day for that. Although I knew this would happen. I told you."

"Yes, you did," Mychal blushed.

"I cannot thank you enough for allowing Luis and I to be a part of this day," Ruby hugged Mychal.

"It would only be right to have my biggest supporters here today. If not for you two, none of this would be happening," she hugged back.

"Now, if we can just get ready for this little one."

"I know," Mychal rubbed her belly, "I have been eating all day to appease him or her, but it feels like real butterflies are in there and the baby is playing with them."

"Oh silly, I am surprised you two

have not slipped up and found out the sex of the baby," the older woman looked skeptical.

"I want to know but he does not. He goes to every appointment so I can't even cheat," Mychal frowned.

"Well quit trying. Be surprised."

She chuckled, "Lately, I am not a fan of surprises."

Before Ruby could reply, the stylist called the bride back to the chair.

"*Señor, un problema! Venga rápidamente!*" Richard heard in his earpiece. He had been nervously moving around for an hour fully dressed. He was so nervous that his shirt was stuck to his back with a thin line of sweat. Only at his soon to be brother-in-law's insistence was he walking around in his lavender vest with an unusual drink on the rocks in his hand. Immediately he snatched up his jacket and barked into his earpiece, "Iroh, stay with Mychal. Not a word. Evan, watch the guests. The same. Max and Tony with me."

Like secret service protecting the president, they wasted no time getting to the security checkpoint. Face dark as a threatening storm cloud, Richard demanded to know what was going on.

Rafael, who was standing by security, spoke first, "That is what I would like to know. I received a hand delivered invitation to your wedding and when I get here, your security will not let me in."

The tall African security guard spoke up, "*Señor*, we explained to you that you are fine. You have an invitation and are on the list. Your guest will not be permitted on the premises for any reason."

The truth of the situation finally dawned on the three newcomers making Richard swear and look around. In a slow and eerily patient voice he asked, "Where is she?"

The same security guard pointed to the small white tent and answered, "Being detained until we got you here before getting the authorities involved. The terms in the order of protection are clear that the *policía* are to be called immediately."

"Authorities? Protection order? What is going on here?" Rafael was shocked.

Richard did not reply as he stormed over to the tent with four men trailing him. He burst through the tent flap barely in control. He stared at Demitri with murderous intent, "How. Dare. You."

Demitri outfitted in a tight and low cut royal blue dress and matching royal blue and white floppy sun hat appeared truly wounded. "Richard, darling, I am so glad that my beloved Rafael and I were invited to share this special day with you. Is everything alright? You appear quite upset. I thought we agreed to disagree and that other little minor understand with your *capulina* was water under the bridge."

"Really? You are a pitiful liar. This is about ruining-"

Rafael cut across him, "What's going on? Demitri, darling, I thought you said that what you had with Richard was over

197

and that he was fine with us dating. You said he knew you were coming to the wedding."

"*Mi Dios*, you have no clue," Richard shot back at his neighbor. "It is obvious that she is lying to you because I do not even care enough to know who she is dating. That disagreement she is trying to downplay was her threatening my pregnant future wife. And this . . . this asinine act was her attempt to ruin our wedding day."

Demitri straightened her back to add poise when she said, "That is not true. I just wanted to accompany my new boyfriend to the wedding of an old friend."

"*Callar perra*!" Richard took a step forward, hands curling into fists. Tony went to grab him while Max stepped in front of him, making Demitri jump back.

Max turned to her and said in a polite voice, "Pardon my friend's emotions as he has got a lot on his mind today. As well as you should, Ms. Salvos. I'm sure you are currently aware of the order of protection the family has in place. You are willfully violating that order now and as a result, the police will be notified for the necessary actions to be taken. I believe they still arrest and jail people in this country for breaking laws."

Rafael was astounded, "Again with the protection order? Who is getting arrested? Demitri?"

Demitri's whole demeanor changed. As if connected to some invisible light switch, gone was the sweet poise and its replacement was a rage monster in a royal blue dress. Her almond colored Mediterranean face with perfect make up flushed crimson and her bulging brown eyes telegraphed hate. She screeched and attempted to lunge at Max. The security guards quickly restrained her, but not her mouth, "You ass! You cannot treat me like some used whore. You will regret this Richard. You, that bitch and that bastard baby!"

Richard wrenched out of Tony's grasp and pushed past Max. He was on Demitri, almost knocking over the security guard on her right. Resisting the urge to choke her by putting his hands behind his back, Richard stopped within inches in front of her and leaned in so their faces were close. It looked as though he was going to brush her cheek with a kiss. The once chaotic situation was now eerily tense with anticipation.

The tent grew quiet so even as low as he spoke everybody heard some part of what he said in angry hushed tones.

"Enough! You crossed the line when you came in here on my wedding day and threatened my wife and unborn child. I am done being mister nice guy. If you ever come near my family again, when they find what is left of you, your soul will already be in hell. And as you well know, I am a man of my word."

When he moved away, Demitri's face was void of color and she licked her lips nervously. As Richard walked toward the exit, all eyes followed him. He paused by Rafael to say, "Stay. Go. Do whatever. Your girlfriend will be leaving with the authorities momentarily."

With a word of gratitude to the security guards, Richard, Tony and Max were gone.

On their way back to the house, the group ran into Luis who was out of breath,

"Where were you? The officiant wants to meet with the groom and groomsmen now."

Richard's entire mood changed. His face brightened as he followed Luis. Impulsively he turned to Tony and Max while speaking into his earpiece, "Not a word to my new wife."

With everyone in the living room, the wedding officiant ran through the ceremony with the groomsmen. Tony showed the officiant the satin blue box he had for the arras coin part of the ceremony. Luis leaned over and whispered in Richard's open, non-occupied ear, "Earpieces? Honestly Richard? We are not protecting the Pope."

The eager groom whispered back, "You have no idea."

After a quick wardrobe check, the five gentlemen were on the way to the alter.

The front lawn of the Garçia-Torrés residence was transformed into an outside paradise. Thirty tables contained family members, coworkers, and business associates. The tables were decorated in royal purple and champagne tablecloths with purple orchids and pale pink lilies in ultra slim vases. A full band was positioned to the left of the platform, playing soft music until Richard and his entourage took their place under the decorated arch. They changed to classical Mozart as Mychal's mother and brother stepped onto the walkway. Max escorted his mother to her table and took his place between Tony and Luis. At the table was a robot monitor with open communication with Mychal's brother Reese and the rest of her family. Richard's cousins, Kendo and

Kumova, Morcheeba's brothers, were at the next table operating the robot's controls.

The wedding was a mixture of American and Spanish traditions. Mychal wanted bridesmaids as one American tradition. When the soft Latin tones began, Ruby walked down the aisle in a pale champagne colored sleeveless chiffon cocktail length dress with a bateau neckline. Riley followed in her matching dress holding the same bouquet of pale pink tulips and purple orchids as Ruby had. Finally, Susanna walked in with a slightly different dress. Her dress was the same color as the two other bridesmaids with the same neckline but her dress had a cowl back that dipped down to her waist and a hemline that was inches above her knee.

In addition to her bouquet, Susanna carried a clear bowl with two lit floating candles. She sat the representation of their parents beside Mychal's mother before taking her place between Ruby and Riley, but not before catching Richard's eye to shoot him a wink. He smiled back.

The music changed to the wedding march as Mychal appeared at the end of the aisle. Seeing her friends and family at the alter caused her to cry as she walked to the archway. By the time she got to the end, the entire wedding party was wiping tears and smiling. To Richard, Mychal floated down the aisle in her off white sleeveless empire waist wedding dress that flattered her curves including the baby bump. He took his handkerchief and dabbed her eyes, making the crowd give a collective sigh. With his own eyes still moist, they began the ceremony. As the officiant talked about the sanctity of marriage and commitment, Richard squeezed her hand.

Before reciting their vows, Tony

handed Richard a blue velvet box big enough to hold a bracelet. Mychal, who had no idea what he was doing, was speechless. He opened and presented Mychal with the traditional thirteen arras coins. Richard's godmother or *madrina* was deceased and her husband, his Uncle Rico, gifted the coins from his family to the couple.

The officiant explained the arras coin tradition for those who were not familiar. He went on to explain the symbolism of the 13 gold coins which meant the groom recognized his responsibility as a provider and pledge of his ability to support and care for his new wife. Her acceptance meant taking his trust and confidence unconditionally with total dedication and prudence. The officiant counted out the 13 coins and placed them in Richard's hands. Each coin represented different values he and Mychal desired to share between themselves: love, harmony cooperation, commitment, peace, happiness, trust, respect, caring, wisdom, joy, wholeness and nurturing. He went on to say the coins were a symbol of their mutual love, fidelity and trust. Then he had Richard repeat after him.

"I, Richard, give you Mychal these thirteen coins as a symbol of my unquestionable trust and confidence I place in you as my beloved wife. As we unite our lives today, I share all material responsibility with you. I pledge these to you with my life. I love you."

At that, fresh tears rolled down her already wet face. She mouthed 'I love you too' and wiped her face. Next, Mychal repeated her part which the officiant had to tell her word for word because she was emotional and did not know the words, "I,

Mychal, accept these coins and assure you of my total love and dedication in looking after you, your possessions and my unconditional love."

Then the officiant said, "In exchanging these coins, Richard and Mychal are conferring, 'what is mine is yours and what is yours is mine.' I bless these coins knowing that they are a symbol of the unlimited good the universe has in store for this loving couple. I accept this for Richard and Mychal, and so it is. *¡Amén!*"

When it came time to recite their vows, Mychal surprised Richard by repeating hers in English and Castilian just as he did. She almost burst into tears at the sight of the beautiful gold and diamond rings he picked out. The whole thing was like a movie that Mychal felt she was watching. She was lost in Richard's smoky green eyes.

"*Señor, puede besar a tu novia,*" the officiant broke her trance.

Richard took Mychal in his arms and kissed her with an urgency that conveyed his love and desire. Mychal lock her arms around his neck and kissed him back with relief and tears. The crowd exploded with applause. He held her and whispered, "I love you so much. *Ustedes son mi vida.*"

She stole a kiss on his cheek, "As are you my husband."

"*Ahora usted está el esposo y la esposa. Me permito presentar, Señor y Señora Roman Ricardo Garçia-Torrés!*"

Guest showered them with white and red rose petals as they walked down the aisle, followed by their wedding party.

The caterer brought out hors d'oeuvres while the wedding party took pictures. Mychal was in such a cloud, she did not notice the photographer or the weird robot during the ceremony. They were taking a series of pictures when Mychal complained she was hungry. Susanna got someone to bring a plate of cheese and shrimp. Mychal thanked none other than Javier Cervantes-Baustista. She broke into a broad grin and hugged him. Richard immediately turned his attention to her, "Who is that?"

Mychal sighed, "If you don't freak out I will tell you."

"Really *Bella*, with everything that has happened today-." then he caught himself. In a softer tone he said, "What I mean is I do not want any surprises to ruin our day."

Mychal dismissed his comment as overprotectiveness, "Calm down and enjoy the day. And let Susanna enjoy it with her new male friend."

Richard gave a mock stunned face to lighten the mood, "Is **that** who that mysterious man is?"

"Yes. And you will leave them alone and concentrate on us today."

He kissed her neck and exposed cleavage, "*Bella* trust me, I want to do that right now."

She laughed and pecked him on the lips before finishing her plate.

The late afternoon wore into night with drinks, food, and partying. Mychal felt like she never danced so much in her life, pregnant or not. She changed from glass slippers to sneakers after pictures, but eventually her ankles began to swell. She sat at the head table while her mother danced with Richard. Max sat beside her to rest.

"Boy, this crowd can party."

Mychal nodded, "Yeah. You should see them at Christmas. They party all day and night."

"You happy sis?"

"God yes! I have never been happier."

He leaned forward, "I'm glad you and Riley are improving."

She made a face. "You and I know how she can be. Her and Reese. I just could not understand her bitterness toward me about this Jacob thing. This was and is his disaster."

Max shook his head, "I know. But she has always had that undercover rivalry with you."

"Undercover? What an understatement."

"Okay, well trying to be undercover rivalry. Mychal, you realize that is what sisters do: fight, make up, one up, and love each other as family."

She started, "But Ma-"

Max cut her off, "That is your childhood issue with our mother. You need to outgrow those childhood issues and soon. Do not, I repeat do not carry that baggage into your new marriage and motherhood. Remember when Gwen almost left me behind similar issues with Ma. Who came over and had this same kind of talk with me?"

"I did," Mychal chuckled remembering talking her sister-in-law into staying and her brother into therapy.

"Now I am returning the favor, dear sister. He is a good guy who cannot wait to be a father." Max hugged her shoulders, "I didn't come over here for all that. I came over here to give you my wedding gift."

Mychal looked puzzled, "Your gift was you came."

"No my dear sister, that was my pleasure. My gift is that I am going to clear your name back home. By the time my niece or nephew comes in this world, this unpleasantness will be mostly taken care of."

She smiled and wiped away a tear, "Thank you bro. Love you."

"And I love you. Now come on and dance with me just once," he pulled her on the floor and they danced until Richard came along to sweep her in his arms for a kiss.

As it got later, the guests were just getting started. They completed the rest of the traditional American activities, garter belt and bouquet tossing. Mychal just gave it to Susanna which made the crowd cheer. After the fireworks display the party goers began anew with lively cultural music as Mychal and Richard slipped upstairs to change clothes and collect their overnight bags. Though their official honeymoon did not start until two weeks after their out of town guest were gone, Richard wanted to do something special for the weekend. They were driving to a cottage resort in Salamanca for the rest of the weekend.

Excitedly and exhausted, they exited through a cascade of bubbles provided by the guest and a machine. Waiting was a white older model BMW convertible sedan,

Mychal gave Richard a questioning look.

"It belongs to Uncle Rico. It was my parents' getaway car for the weekends before he bought it from my dad. I thought it was appropriate," he held her door open.

"Ah, husband, you are full of surprises," she teased.

Richard got in the car and started it, "Says the person who has been the biggest surprise since the day she walked through my door."

Mychal laughed, "Yeah, remember you almost threw me out. Poor Pedro."

Richard smiled at the memory as they turned on the road and began their honeymoon weekend.

Susanna relaxed immediately as her brother disappeared down the drive. She went back to the party and enjoyed being with Javier. They danced and drank more than Susanna intended. Long after the guest left and the household was asleep, she and Javier stayed up talking, eventually falling asleep watching television in the family room. The next day after she changed, they were eating wedding leftovers when Javier asked why she had not told her older brother about them.

Susanna shrugged, "Richard is going through a lot right now. He worries about me unnecessarily like I am still a child. I am a grown woman but it was not until Mychal came along that I really grew into my own."

He looked at Susanna surprised, "How so?"

"I was busy trying to be who the family wanted me to be. My aunts and cousins wanted me to be like them but they are so aristocratic and self-absorbed. I grew up seeing my mother who was kind and refined to the point of being docile. She let my father make most of the decisions for the family. But when she wanted something she usually got her way," Susanna smiled at the recollections. "But Mychal was and is nothing like that. She is so aggressive. Wait, not aggressive, she is confident. She knows what she wants and is driven to get it. She has done so much to be thirty-two. I just turned twenty-four and still live at home."

"But you are in school. It should be okay to stay home while attending college."

"Javier I know, but I want to be independent. I want to work for my own money, not have my brother monitor my trust fund. I even thought about living in the dorm before Richard decided to move Tony and me into the *suegra* wing."

Javier looked uncomfortable, "You have an extra wing in this house?"

"Well it was where my grandparents stayed when they got too old to care for themselves. My parents had it built so they would be closer to family and be cared for daily. It has a walkway to the garage and a private entrance from the grounds. Almost like my own apartment," Susanna sounded pleased.

Javier shifted nervously looking at his hands.

Susanna noticed the drop in

conversation, "Javier what's wrong?"

He looked away, "I never knew you had such a, um, different lifestyle."

She was puzzled, "I do not understand what you mean by 'different lifestyle'."

"Your family is financially stable," he tried without calling her wealthy.

"Javé, my family is a working family. My parents set it up so we all could go to school and not have our studies distracted by work. Richard went to school in Miami, Florida and Tony messed around for a few years taking some business classes at the American University. My brothers work every day at the family's shipping business. I chose to use my trust money as income so I could volunteer at impoverished schools to teach piano and violin," she went to hug him. "Do not let how my family earns a living bother you. You liked me before you found out about all this, right?"

He stuttered, "Yes . . . but that was before all this."

Susanna moved back and spread her arms out, "Again, you liked the person I was before what you call 'all this'. Have I changed in the last twenty-four hours? Or two hours for that matter?"

"I guess not."

"Then what my family does or has, does not change who I am." Javier nodded as though he agreed with her statement so she continued, "I am the same *niña* that you took to the grape fields on a lazy Sunday. The same *niña* that danced with you all night and crashed on the sofa. Look Javé, I am the same person."

He looked at her with eyes that said something beyond acceptance, "You are right, you are the same person. A beautiful person inside and out."

With slow motion moves, Javier pulled Susanna in his arms and blazed her lips with a kiss. Their tongues met as his hand roamed her petite curves in her jeans. His lips left hers to kiss her jawline up to her ear where he tickled her earlobe with his tongue.

Susanna felt herself losing control. The man's tongue was keeping her focused on him. He went from her ear to recapture her mouth. His hand dipped inside her jeans as his palms caressed her bare bottom. His moves sent a pulse through Susanna as she could envision his hands touching other places. Her lips left his so she could taste his throat. She wanted him out of his shirt. She wanted to see his muscles exposed to her touch. She wanted all of him to be hers.

"*Wow*, I think my eyes are bleeding. No wait, one just fell out and rolled under the kitchen island . . . which is great by the way because I prefer blindness to seeing this," Max interrupted them. "Richard's little sister making out in the kitchen on a Sunday morning. Did you contaminate the counter with anything other than coffee? All I want is some coffee. Can I just get some coffee?"

Amused at his absurd teasing, Susanna turned to Max, not letting go of Javier's hand, "Oh ha ha. Of course you can get coffee silly."

"I'm Max," he extended his hand to Susanna's friend, "Newest family member and witness to you being held against your will in the kitchen."

"Javier," the younger man shook it with his free hand.

"Nice to meet you, even though Susanna clearly has you isolated in the kitchen to take advantage of you," Max teased even more.

"Max!"

"Just kidding," he poured a mug of coffee. Before walking outside Max said, "Carry on."

Slightly embarrassed, Susanna pulled Javier into her arms for another kiss.

8
Departures and Discoveries

Mychal and Richard's honeymoon was scheduled for two weeks after the actual wedding. They came home Monday afternoon to spend time with her family before they left on Tuesday. Mychal was excited to tell them about their cottage in the country. She showed them some pictures from her phone. She felt like she did not have enough words to tell them what a wonderful time they had walking through the countryside with nights of fireworks in and out of the sheets. Both she and Richard hated for it to end, but Mychal knew he had things going on at work. Plus, her family was going home and with her own situation back in New York there was no telling when she would see them again. Monday afternoon was spent picking out baby items with her mother and sister. In the evening, both families sat together at Mychal's favorite restaurant near campus enjoying their last few hours together.

Once back at home, Richard, Mychal and Max stayed up talking while everyone else went to bed. When Mychal called it a night, Max and Richard discussed the things that neither wanted to say in front of her. Richard assured his brother-in-law that after the incident at the wedding, his ex-girlfriend would not be a problem. He also assured Max that with their wedding done, he planned to pass more work duties over to Tony and concentrate on making sure all preparations were done for the baby's arrival.

Max told Richard his plans to take a more assertive tactical approach to Mychal's fraud and tax problems. So far he had let events play out with Riley's husband, but once home he wanted to take a more forceful position on the case. He wanted to resolve this problem for the new couple so they could welcome their newest family member without any worries. Both men fell asleep while talking in the family room.

The next morning both Mychal and Richard rode to the airport with the family. It was going to be tough for her dealing with their departure and Richard knew she needed support. Mychal was in tears when saying goodbye to her mother and sister, but really cried when she hugged her brother. Richard felt sad as well saying goodbye to his new favorite relative. The two men hugged briefly before Max went through security.

On the way home Mychal was quiet, so Richard held her hand, often commenting on little things to break the tension. He telephoned Tony with his decision to stay home with his despondent wife. Her mood improved when they ate and walked the dog. Impulsively, Richard suggested they put the baby's crib together. His idea worked. By the time they were attaching the front panel, he was cursing and sweating while Mychal laughed at his clumsy actions. By dinner the crib was together and the baby's room was nearly finished. While she cleaned up the dinner dishes, they talked about how setting up the room made the whole situation seem surreal. After feeding and walking the dog, both Mychal and Richard went to bed, exhausted from an emotional day and lack of sleep.

The next day was business as usual. Richard went to the office and Mychal went to campus. The end of the first summer semester was a little over a week away, followed by overlapping sessions of summer school. She was in her office grading items in the course's electronic grade book drop box when Ruby paid her a visit. Mychal got up to hug her.

"Oh no sit down," the older woman waved her off.

"I am glad to see you," Mychal smiled.

"Me too. Dearheart, I cannot thank you enough for allowing Luis and I to share your day."

"Ruby I would not have had my special day without you and Luis. You guys talked me into staying in the area for my baby with or without Richard."

Ruby gave Mychal an 'oh really' face and said, "We all knew it was going to be 'with Richard'."

Mychal gave her friend a sheepish grin.

"We really had a blast. Your family is very comical, not at all like you described them."

Mychal smirked, "They were on their best behavior because they wanted me married off. When they got here I had a talk with Riley. Then Max had a few talks with me about our mother. He suggested that I not take the past with her into my future with my family. He was right."

"I am so glad somebody talked some sense into you." Ruby changed the subject,

"Susanna's new friend is too cute."

"He sure is. I had to say something to Richard at the wedding. He was going to ruin her fun on our wedding day."

"Always the older brother," Ruby chuckled.

"Yeah, but he needs to let go," Mychal sighed. "Richard is not that way with Tony at all. I understand we are from different cultures, but I want him to lighten up and let her live her own life. I need him to stop being her secondary father and shift his focus to becoming a parent in our own new life."

The older woman frowned, "I did not get the impression he is lacking in his pre fatherly duties. He goes to every appointment, he made sure you had protection and he even has gone with you to buy baby clothes. What exactly do you want?"

"I want him to shift his focus from micromanaging his little sister to preparing for his new baby. He has enough to worry about with his mess at his company. Honestly, I was hoping that issue would clear up before the baby comes," Mychal sighed again.

Ruby immediately understood. "This is not about his sister per se, you are worried about him. You think if he leaves her life alone that will lessen his stress."

"I think so."

"Has anything new happened? Last time you mentioned anything, there was a big incident on the docks."

Mychal shook her head negative, "That could have been a disaster. If that forklift had actually blown up, everything could have been lost. That was the first time something deadly almost happened."

Ruby leaned in to ask, "There were other incidents?"

"There were, but he did not tell me until I got Iroh. Richard said that his car was vandalized in the garage a month before he realized the incidents might be related. One or two flat tires really doesn't faze guys. When he came out one night and all the windows were smashed, then he said he knew the tires were not an accident. He moved his car to another space and by the end of the week the car was scratched up with some kind of red chemical poured on the seats. Richard claimed he did not want to tell me because I might get upset to the point it would bother the baby."

"He might be right."

Mychal rolled her eyes, "Whatever. Richard is always being overprotective. After that he changed to an unmarked space, switched to driving the Range Rover and hired security."

"Vandalism is petty and vengeful. I wondered what prompted him to hire security. Last semester was fine."

"Before the car incidents, there were some little accidents at the job site. Then there was the big thing with the fleet of work trucks that were somehow tampered with during the route. The company has insurance but still lost somewhere in the low six figures." Mychal paused then said, "None of this happened before I came to stay. I feel like a walking curse to the family or something."

Ruby waved off her notion, "Stop being silly. Sometimes bad things happen to good people. Besides, now you are a part of that family, curse and all."

"True. The stuff at work until the forklift incident I could agree with, but the car; that's personal," Mychal almost seemed to be talking to herself not Ruby.

"Was anybody else's car vandalized?"

Nearly in a daze she replied, "No and Richard mentioned Tony's car was right beside his."

"Then that sounds personal. Does Richard have any enemies?" Ruby asked.

"I really don't know. He has not said anything about enemies or rival companies. His family is close and he has a solid business reputation."

"Well dear, I am sure Richard has

this under control," the older woman rose to leave, "tell him we want to spend time with you two before the baby comes. I am sure he will work us in the schedule."

Mychal collected her purse and keys to walk out with Ruby who asked, "Where are you going?"

"To surprise my husband," she said. As they walked down the hall past the student lounge she called, "Come on Iroh, let's go."

He appeared out of nowhere, hurrying to keep up with Mychal who was on a mission.

At Richard's office she waved at the security guard and secretary, then walked in his office before the other woman could get off the phone. Richard and Tony were sitting at his conference table looking at something on a monitor. Richard stood up and smiled uneasy when he saw Mychal.

"*Bella*, what are you doing here?"

She shamelessly walked over and kissed her husband passionately on the mouth. His surprise was an ego booster. "I came to discuss an idea with you."

"I love that you came all this way for a kiss and an idea, but right now? Could it wait until we got home?"

"I can leave," Tony started to rise.

"No, I need you in on this. And Evan too," she motioned for him to sit as she stood beside Richard. He was both confused and intrigued. He called his head of security who was in his own office. Once the three men were in place Mychal began, "Honey, remember telling me about the garage incidents?"

"Oh this again. Mychal do not worry about-"

She cut him off, "Oh I am not worried but I need you to play along with me. So you told me that the first incident was tires being cut or slashed, right?"

"Yes."

"But Tony's car was right beside yours." She turned to Tony, "Anything wrong with your car bro?"

He looked puzzled at Mychal, "No."

"Next you tell me the windows were shattered and nobody heard a thing even though the car has an alarm. Right?"

Richard was starting to get

concerned, "Mychal, where are you going with this?"

"Let her play this out," Evan leaned in fascinated.

She answered Richard by asking Tony, "Were you parked beside him that day?"

He thought a minute before answering, "No, I was at the docks that day."

"So the day the vandalism got worse your car was not beside his? Possibly alerting the person that Richard was in the office alone?" Mychal asked.

"I guess," Tony confirmed her suspicions.

"That last time when the car really got damaged, where was Tony's Maserati?

Was that messed up at all? Any of that red paint get splashed on your car?"

"It was right beside mine. And no, not one drop of paint, no scratches, no flat tires and no smashed windshield. Nothing," Richard remembered.

"I think I see where you are going," Evan chimed in.

"Have you fired anybody lately or hired anybody new? Or how about outbidding any rival companies in business?"

Richard's attention was piqued more than ever, "We do not handle human resource matters. We contract that area of business to outside companies. Why?"

"Because the stuff that was done to your car was petty," she replied. "Pettiness is the work of females and cowards. Angry frustrated men confront and challenge the person causing them problems. Females and cowards are sneaky. They will not confront a bigger threat, but will get their revenge in other ways, especially for a brother, husband or boyfriend. If somehow you make them lose money from the household, embarrass or insult them, their revenge will make sure you lose something equally as important like spending money to replace damage items or loss of reputation."

Richard and Tony just looked at Mychal bewildered. Evan just smiled at her astute points.

"Hello? Feedback?" she snapped her fingers. "You two are looking at me like I just grew blue fur and levitated off the floor."

Tony spoke first, "I will contact the

human resources company and have them check on any terminations or layoffs."

Evan was up and moving, "As soon as you get that list I will have my team check those individuals out before turning names over to the authorities."

Richard gave Mychal a hug and whispered in her ear, "You are amazing."

"Thank you honey."

"Right now I am so turned on," he kissed her ear while his hands rubbed her back.

"Oh no sir," she said firmly, "you have work to do."

"I could work on my husbandly duties right now." Richard shifted her so he could press himself against her thigh. His head dipped so he could kiss her cleavage.

Richard's actions were starting to break down Mychal's resolve. Before Tony came in and found her in a comprising position on the conference table she said, "As fun as that sounds, Tony will be back soon. Besides I have a better idea. Why don't you finish a little early here while I go home and make some baked ziti with a fresh salad and homemade zeppoles?"

"My birthday is not until our honeymoon and I still get a meal like that?" he teased.

"No, but it will give me time for a cold shower and you time to refocus. The sooner we get this problem resolved, the sooner we get on with our lives."

Richard rested his forehead against hers, "What did I do to deserve you?"

"You let me stay and saved me from that vicious attack houseplant," Mychal gave him a quick kiss. "Because I know you are working hard, I have another surprise at home."

"Stop teasing and just go," he waved her out. "Tell Tony to hurry up before I leave with you."

Richard waited until Evan returned to discuss Mychal's notion in greater detail. When his brother came back to the table, they brainstormed how the garage incidents and the dock incident could be related. Tony contacted the building security to inquire about any video footage while Richard contacted the company attorney about any possible lawsuits or allegations from other lawyers in the past six months to a year.

Mychal stopped to get her

ingredients for dinner at a local market. As she cooked, the baby turned and kicked. Her mind drifted to wondering if the baby was a boy or girl. She was snapped out of her daydreaming by the dogs barking and running toward the back of the property. Solomon raced to the door, barking as they ran past the patio door in the direction of the wall behind the pool.

"What is it boy?"

The dog just whined and paced in front of the door. Slightly unnerved, Mychal continued to make the batter for the zeppoles. Iroh came by the patio doors in the kitchen and gave her a thumbs up sign. She returned the gesture, breathing a sigh of relief, for once believing that having security was a good idea. She settled down and finished her dinner, stopping only to text Susanna to ask if she wanted to come to dinner.

As expected she got: `No with Javé` ☺

Mychal was loading the dishwasher when Richard came home. His face was tired and sported a frown when he walked in the kitchen.

"Richard?"

He responded by giving her a smile. He crossed the room to give her a hug and kiss. "Dinner smells good and you look sexy in this kitchen."

"Well everything is ready. I just need you."

"Let me drop my bag in the study and change," Richard headed toward his study.

"A package came for you today. It is from Max."

Mychal was delighted that her order came before their honeymoon. She opened the box and retrieved her new titanium expanding baton. It was so lightweight and popped out with the slightest flick of her wrist. The silver metal had a blueish tint with textured handle. It collapsed into less than ten inches and came with an ankle holster.

On his way back through the kitchen Richard stopped to marvel at his wife's new weapon. Nonchalantly Mychal asked, "Did you talk with Iroh today?"

He paused, then carefully chose his words, "Yes he called and told me the dogs found a child's toy against the back wall."

She was puzzled, "A child's toy? How did that happen?"

He dismissed her inquiry with a

shrug, "Maybe it fell out of one of the workers' trucks. The painters were here on Monday finishing the trim work in Susanna and Tony's apartment."

"Oh."

"Let me change *Bella*, I'm hungry," Richard went upstairs trying to avoid further conversation. He did not want to lie to his wife about the fact that the stuffed animal had on stained baby clothes. He was not certain if the object was a strange coincidence or a threat to Mychal.

Their dinner was just what Richard needed after the events of the day. He really enjoyed her cooking and talked with her about the origin of certain baby names in the Spanish culture. Mychal surprised him by discussing her thoughts on how finishing the apartment would make Susanna and Tony more independent. She also suggested he get to know his little sister's boyfriend. For once, Richard agreed. He cleared the dishes and stored the food when she let the dog out. He quickly joined her outside for safety.

Upstairs Mychal practically made Richard soak in the tub while she washed his hair. On the bed, she toweled him off and massaged his body until she heard him snoring softly. Satisfied, she pulled up the covers, turned off the lights and eased in bed beside him.

The evening with Mychal and the weekend gave Richard the energy he needed to attack the problems at work with new stamina. They were leaving for their honeymoon Thursday so he had three days to work with security to find the person he believed to be a vandal and possible saboteur.

By Monday afternoon he, Tony and Evan, had the list from human resources cut in half. Tuesday Mychal had a doctor's appointment to be cleared for flight. She measured within weight and size for thirty weeks and the baby was developing well. Mychal was advised to watch her own weight as the baby would gain the most weight in the last trimester. The doctor advised any extra weight would just make her uncomfortable, which Richard noted. On the way to dropping him off at the office he also noted that her growing belly was touching the steering wheel in the Porsche. Richard made up his mind that she needed a different vehicle.

Wednesday looked to be a busy day for them both. That morning he told

Mychal it was time for her to change cars

"Is the Porsche broken?"

"No, but I think you might be more comfortable in something with a real backseat and four doors."

She did not argue, "Okay."

Richard was pleasantly surprised, "Okay? Where is the 'not my Porsche honey' speech?"

"Well, they do not really accommodate baby seats. I will drive the Porsche on our date nights after the baby gets here."

He nodded his head in agreement, "Fair enough."

"Try to come home early. I need help to make sure we pick a place for your birthday and packing," she said firmly.

"My birthday. Ooh yeah that is next Tuesday. I thought I just might wear my American birthday suit," he grinned.

Mychal raised an eyebrow, "Early please."

"Fine. Enjoy your last day with the Porsche. After we get back from Thailand, please use the truck or Bentley from now on. Or you could just let Iroh drive you places."

"Yes sir," she hurried him out to the garage so they could get the day started. Mychal pecked him on the lips and said, "Early please."

"For you *Bella*, anything."

9

Collisions and Honesty

Susanna was glad to see Mychal and Richard leave the house. Although their apartment was done and some of she and Tony's belongings were moved in last weekend, Susanna wanted to spend the next ten days enjoying her new found freedom. She also wanted Javier to spend the week with her. Her first order of business was buying furniture for their living room. Susanna shared her plans with her twin when she stopped by the office Friday. "*Hola hermano*, what are you doing?"

"Getting ready to meet with security in about 20 minutes. What are you doing here? Is something wrong?" Tony frowned.

"No, I need a favor." Tony raised his eyebrow inquisitively because his sister never asked for any favors. She continued, "Can you stay at the house while Mychal and Richard are gone?"

"I thought **you** were staying at the house while they were gone. Where are you going?"

She smirked, "Nowhere silly, I just want to spend time with Javier."

Tony teased, "You want him to spend time at the house. Look at you blushing and in love."

Susanna blushed again and her brother burst into laughter.

"So will you do it?"

"Sure, but you will owe me."

She feigned shock, "How do I owe you? Remember Ava and the time Richard blamed me for leaving you at that party? Remember Sophia and I covered for you with him?"

Tony smiled at the memories of his sister covering for him so he could spend the night with different females. Her actions kept Richard from delivering his usual sermons about the family name and image.

Susanna was not done, "Or how about with Cassandra? When her husband came to the house-"

"Okay, okay, I said I would do it."

"But you cannot tell Richard he

255

spent the week."

Tony's whole face changed with that revelation, "Oh I see now. You want to play house with him in the apartment. That is why you need me to stay at the house."

"Absolutely. Now that Iroh is not in the house, I need you there for security and Javé will guard my body," she quipped.

"Gross sis. I did not need to hear that," he put his finger in his right ear.

"Oh please, your room was across from mine growing up. I endured much more than words. The music didn't drown out everything."

"Damn, you did not miss a thing," he huffed.

"Whatever. I am looking for living room furniture today. Anything in particular you just must have in my choices?" Susanna asked.

"Something in dark orange and tan with some splashes of red. And a big television like 70 inches or larger. Sony or Samsung. Sis, I also like plants and a liquor cabinet, preferably leather and oak with-"

She cut him off, "If you need all this then perhaps you should come with me."

Tony frowned, "Love to, but someone has to catch this vandal slash saboteur. I would like to have at least a name when our brother and his wife get back."

"Any more incidents?"

He sat back in his chair, "Not since the stuffed animal in baby clothes last week."

Susanna gasped, "What! When? Why did you keep something like this from me? Did Richard tell Mychal? What is going on?"

Tony shrugged, "Well I did not tell you because Richard did not know if the incident was a threat or a coincidence. He told Mychal part of the truth and as for what is going on . . . I wish I knew. All I do know is that someone is trying to ruin this company. Everything seems to be centered on Richard. When his car got vandalized-"

"What! When did that happen?" she practically shouted.

"Some time ago," her brother continued, "but as I said, his car was trashed and mine was untouched. Then there was the straps being cut on various small containers making the cargo arrive damaged and the rats in the clothing containers. Let's not forget the work truck shipment that we took a serious hit on. Finally, that dock incident could have killed someone. So we did not want to overreact to a child's toy that may have fallen out of a worker's truck."

"When did you say that happened?" Susanna asked brows furrowed in confusion.

"Last Wednesday."

Still in thought she said, "No workers were at the apartment last week. Mychal's family left Tuesday. Pedro was there Wednesday supervising removal of decorations off the lawn and planting flowers around the apartment. He does not have small kids. Where did security find it?"

"Adjacent to the wall behind the

pool house."

She gave Tony a skeptical face, "That was an odd place. Wonder what is on the other side of the wall."

Wearily, he replied, "I don't know. Like I said, weird things like that make a person wonder whether it was an accident or not."

"Well I have to get to the stores if I want to find something before the weekend," Susanna needed to leave.

"Remember my colors," Tony called after her.

Susanna shopped with the new information from her twin in the back of her mind. Though distracted, she was able to find a set of furniture that fit her idea of how she wanted their shared living room to look and had Tony's required colors. She texted him pictures and his response was a smiley face. With the delivery set for the next morning, she made her next stop a plant nursery.

Susanna purchased two large indoor palm plants and four smaller plants that had orange colored blossoms. She took home the smaller plants and arranged to come back for the larger ones later. On her way home, she got a text from Javier asking did she want to go to a wine tasting that evening. She texted back yes and hurried home to change.

The next day Susanna was excited. She called to talk to Javier about the incident at the house last week and how she wanted him to stay with her for safety purposes. He immediately agreed. That was one of the things she loved about him, his acceptance of her and her current chaotic family life. After breakfast she got a

call from security that the furniture
company was cleared and on their way
back to the apartment. Susanna downed
her juice and headed out to meet the truck.

By late afternoon everything,
furniture wise, was set up in the apartment
including her bedroom. She paid the
delivery men extra to move her bedroom
furniture to the apartment. Pedro picked
up her indoor palms and helped Susanna
place them for optimal lighting in the living
room and small sun parlor off from the
entry. Together they reassembled her
vanity and moved the last of her personal
items from the main house to the
apartment. By the time the sun was going
down, she was tired. The evening was
finished by Javier bringing takeout,
watching a movie, and both falling asleep
on the couch.

Sunday morning they made a trip to the main house for breakfast. They spent from mid-morning to afternoon at the pool. As they lounged, Susanna thought it was a good time to talk openly.

"Javé, I need you to help me while my brother is gone, but it might inconvenience you."

"How?"

Susanna hesitated.

"What is it?" he prompted, wading to the edge of the pool.

She sighed, "There are some things going on with my family that I have been keeping from you because I thought if I told you . . . you would leave me."

"Leave you?" Javier hoisted himself

out of the pool to sit beside her on the pool's edge. "What is so bad that I would leave the love of my life?"

Susanna was shocked and happy at the same time. She managed to say, "The love of your life?"

"*Si* Susanna. I love you and nothing would make me leave you."

She hesitated again, "But how can you love me? I feel like you just got to know me and half the time we spend together I am trying to keep you from *mi familia loca*."

Javier heard the anxiety in her voice. He had to retrace his steps and say something that would not add to her anxiousness. "Okay slow down. Maybe I did not say what I meant. I am trying to say that I am falling in love with you. You may not have feelings as strong as mine, but I know you care deeply for me as well. As far as your family . . . they are different. Your twin is a *canalla* and your older brother is, well, overprotective and *mandón*. But in whatever situation that requires all those guards, I believe he is protecting something that means the world to him, his family."

"But Javé that is what I am trying to say. It is something more than just protecting his family," Susanna replied. She went on to tell him everything about what had happened since Mychal moved in. She told him about the name mix up, how her brother had fallen for his new wife, and how Mychal had advocated for her with Richard several times. She continued by telling him about the blow up between Demitri and Mychal, when they all found out Mychal was pregnant, and that she had legal troubles back in the States. Susanna finished with the visits Demitri paid to her new sister-in-law at the college and the incidents that happened at the docks, forcing her brother to hire security. Once she was done she held her breath waiting for Javier to say something.

Moments went by before he said, "That **is** a lot to deal with. At first I thought he had security because he did not like me."

Susanna gave him a baffled look and Javier began to laugh. She relaxed a little and remarked, "At least my family's status is not a problem anymore."

He smirked, "It was a problem in the beginning, but the fact that you and your family do not act like the money makes you better than everyone else changed my opinion. At the wedding I expected everyone to look down their noses and be unfriendly snobs like at those wine tasting charity events we go to sometimes. It was the best wedding I have ever attended and I had a super time. As I said, I understand why your brother has gone to such lengths to protect his family. Now that I know, I feel the same way about protecting you, someone I am starting to love."

Susanna blushed, "Javier, I want to love you, but I feel whatever is going on right now does not allow me to give us the time needed to explore our feelings."

He put his arm around her shoulders and kissed her cheek, "This situation will not last forever. I am not going anywhere, so when things settle down, we will have all the time we need."

His touch made her feel safe and created butterflies in her stomach. "Javé, thank you for understanding. I felt on edge since the guards came. I feel like I keep you from this house to keep you from this mess. That's why I am always at your apartment or we are always out. This week I really wanted us to spend time alone in my new place. No Tony and no security, just us."

He gave her a whimsical look, "How has what you told me changed your plans for 'just us'?"

Susanna smiled, "Now that you are not running scared, I guess my plans are still on."

"I would not have it any other way," Javier said before deciding it was time to open up to her and tell her his own hidden truth.

It took Javier a minute to compose himself and look at her. He hoped his eyes did not show the emotional turmoil that had suddenly risen to take over the moment. Finally he said, "I have something I need to share with you and hope you do not run scared."

"That sounds serious, what is it?" she sounded worried.

He let out a breath and began, "There is a lot you have to learn about me. My past is . . . difficult."

Susanna held his hand and said, "You can trust me. Javier, we cannot go any further as a couple if you do not trust me enough to share your past."

Her indication that she wanted them to go further as a couple made his heart skip and gave Javier hope that she might actually understand. So he trudged on and said, "Señor Plasençia is more than my boss, he is like my father. He rescued me from a church orphanage as a young teenager and made me part of his family. His children were grown and leaving the home when he and Mama Rosa took me in."

Lost in memory he continued, "I was on the streets stealing stuff to give out to kids at the orphanage so they would like me. I tried to steal from him and he caught me. Instead of turning me in to the authorities, he went to the sisters and came up with a plan that I would work with him every day to keep me off the streets. After months of working with him and his wife, they asked if I wanted to live with them instead of the orphanage. I said yes and it was the best decision of my life."

"Javier I had no idea you were an orphan. You talk about your mother all the time," Susanna was puzzled.

"She died when I was ten. After she died I tried to live with my father for a year or so. But I was the bastard child of a rich and powerful man whose budding career and image meant more to him than me. It did not help that his wife was not comfortable with the child of his mistress living under her roof especially when she was trying to have her own children," he shifted uncomfortably. "I was enrolled in private schools as my father's nephew and threatened into secrecy. After I got kicked out of my fourth private school, my father took me to stay with the nuns and I never saw him again."

"Javier that is an awful way to treat a child. Did you work things out with your father before he died?"

"Susanna, I did not say my father was dead. I see him every six months or so at various charity functions. Sometimes he

271

speaks sometimes he looks down his nose and does not acknowledge me. It depends on which crowd of people he is with at the time. If his wife is with him, he never speaks," he smiled dryly at the memory of their brief meetings.

"But you said-"

Javier cut her off, "I know I said he was dead but honestly he is dead to me. The family I really love and recognize are the wonderful people who cared for me , Mama Rosa and Papa José Plasençia."

Susanna chose her words carefully, "So your father must be some wealthy and powerful man?"

"Only to himself and the people who do not know that he is capable of throwing away his own child to protect his career and himself," Javier sounded bitter.

"That is why you freaked out at the wedding when you found out we were as you said, 'financially stable'." She paused then added, "And I proved to you that all people with inherited money are not like your father."

"Oh, you are nothing like them. You are like no one I have ever met in my life and I like the way you make me feel," his eyes echoed his words.

Susanna blushed at his comment and smiled, "I like the way you make me feel too. Like a real woman, not some silly little sister and teenage girl."

"Trust me, I know you are all woman," Javier said before pulling her into a smoldering kiss.

After dinner they went by his place to pick up clothes for a few days. Back at her apartment they played Mahjong and drank wine. With courage bolstered by wine, Susanna suggested that they retire upstairs instead of sleeping on the sofa another night. Once upstairs her nerves were slightly rattled by the thought she never spent the night with a man in her bed.

Javier came out the bathroom dressed in gym shorts and a t-shirt. He looked at Susanna and said, "I understand the sofa but do you sleep in your own bed fully clothed?"

She blushed, "I normally sleep in a t-shirt and boy shorts."

"Do not let my presence change that. I will not do anything other than hold you," he grinned. "Unless you want me to do something more?"

"Javé," she called over her shoulder heading into the bathroom, "always a gentleman."

When she came out he was watching TV. Shyly, Susanna slid under the covers beside him to cuddle. They watched television in awkward silence. Though she was comfortable in his embrace, she was a nervous ball of excitement and anticipation. Javier shifted his arm causing her to turn so she could ask was something wrong. When she saw the hungry passion in his eyes, Susanna knew she was lost.

Javier moved to kiss her, only brushing her lips. Susanna pulled him in to deepen the kiss and explore his mouth. He rolled them onto her back and parted her legs with his knee. In response she bent her leg so she could feel the rigidness beneath his shorts grinding against her. She moaned as his lips left hers to taste her neck. Javier propped up on one arm to take his shirt off. Susanna quickly helped him then discarded her own. She inhaled sharply as his lips touched her bare breast and his fingers slipped inside her boy shorts pajama bottoms to stroke the burning peak between her thighs. Susanna arched her back each time his tongue and fingers touched her. Javier looked up and asked, *"¿Te gusta cuando me toque usted?"*

"Sí quiero más," she responded.

He trailed kisses down her mid-section while working on her boy shorts. Javier's eyes drank in the sight of her petite naked frame, making her blush. His hand went in his pocket, both fishing for its contents and pulling his shorts off. In moments, he joined their bodies making Susanna moan loudly. He pushed up her leg so he could caress her supple bottom and pull her closer to deeply fulfill her desires. Slowly and sensuous at first, their movements quickened fueled by the need to please the other person. Susanna dug her nails in his back relaying her intensity and urging Javier to continue pleasing her. Their pace became harried before he leaned over and whispered in her ear, "¡*Ahora mi amor! ¡Dése a mí*!"

Like magic words, Susanna exclaimed his name, hips jerking and mind clouded. Her uncontrollable movements were too much for Javier. He pulled her into a tight embrace and after a minute more of his punctuated movements that seemed to telegraph his raw emotions, finally Javier whispered his love while still cradled in her arms. After forever, he rolled on his side and adjusted Susanna in his arms.

"Javier *que fue increíble*. I . . . I," her words failed.

He kissed her forehead, "I wanted to please you. You are so wonderful and I wanted our first time to be unforgettable."

Susanna chuckled, "Is that to say every time will not be like that?"

Javier frowned, "I did not say-"

She cut him off, "As a matter of fact I think I would like to see if we can do a repeat act. But this time it is I that will please you."

He grinned, "*Usted piensa que sí*?"

Susanna threw him a wicked grin, "Let me show you my love."

She rolled him on his back and proceeded to spend the rest of the night driving him to the edge of insanity with her tongue and hips.

"You do not have to check on me every day," Tony said to his sister the next night. "Have fun with Javier. I am fine being in the house with the dog."

She sighed, "I know, I guess I feel a little guilty that's all. I also keep your safety in the back of my mind."

"*Dejen de mentir*, you do not feel guilty. Every morning you come to the house with that silly grin on your face after Javier goes to work," he made his sister blush. "As for safety, I am grown and can handle myself."

"Okay, I will stop smothering you. Where are you going tonight?"

"Out with Yadira, the nice secondary school chemistry teacher that I met when I had car trouble at the market Friday. She showed me how to clean my battery cables with soda then jump started the car," he grinned like a crazy man.

Susanna gave him a worried look, "What's wrong with your car? You could have called me."

"*Hermana*, thanks for the concern, but I had a pretty redhead who had all the right curves with brains helping me with my car. She even told me what might be keeping the battery from getting a full charge." Tony grinned, "That was so hot. I asked her out and she said yes."

His sister replied, "What? She can walk and chew gum at the same time? *Hermano*, what's going on? Your girls are all cup size and no common sense."

280

"Well to get different results, you have to do something different. Besides the other girls were just something to do. This one is unique. She is a real woman," he sounded distracted. "So while my car is down I will drive Mychal's Porsche. Richard wants her to drive the Bentley for the rest of her pregnancy anyway."

"I know she hated that."

Snagging the keys, Tony said, "Surprisingly, she agreed. Anyway, have fun tonight. Tell Javé he needs to get all his nightly escapades in before I come back to the apartment Wednesday."

Susanna was so shocked at her brother's comment that she could not say something smart back at him before he left.

Before pulling out of the drive, Tony texted his date and adjusted the seat. He never realized Mychal was shorter than him because her presence always made her appear larger than life. He had to adjust her taste in music too because it sounded like something in a rave party blasting out of the speakers. He was synching up the car's Bluetooth to his phone and did not notice the vehicle behind him. Focusing on the dash and his phone he did not see the black truck turn off its headlights. Checking the time Tony sped up in the light rain to get to the restaurant on time to impress this new girl he was unusually attracted to. He did not see the truck match his speed and start to pass him. The truck suddenly veered sharply to the right, colliding hard with the Porsche's left rear quarter panel.

Tony was caught completely off guard when the contact of another vehicle caused the car to spin left. The tires could not grip the wet pavement enough, forcing the back end into a fishtail spin. He tried to turn in the direction of the spin then correct, but the road conditions and speed were too much. The car did another complete spin before ending up skidding off the road into a ditch facing the opposite direction. The trees growing in the ditch stopped the Porsche's motion but not before branches smashed the side windows, one impaling Tony's hand as he threw up his right hand and turned his head to avoid the shattering glass. He gripped the steering wheel with one hand for dear life as the car finally died.

Tony's breath came in harsh pants as he tried to clear his head. He needed to call for help but had no idea where his phone got thrown. Still disoriented by the crash, Tony slowly became aware of the pain in his right hand. He turned to see the reason his hand would not move, only to come face to face with the tip of the branch merely inches from his face. When he tried to move his hand fresh pain erupted. Trying to calm his now frazzled nerves, he debated whether to pull the branch out of his hand. He tried the door with his free hand and it opened. Relief washed over Tony. Still gathering his wits, he looked around for his cell phone to call emergency services. Before he could, a man from a stopped car approached him.

"Se le da bien?"

"No, necesito ayuda. Por favor Llame al 112."

"Mi esposa llam. Creo que salir del coche, no parecen seguros," the stranger replied.

Tony snapped off the tree branch tip

then reached on around his hand to see if
he could break the branch. Slowly he
moved his hand and bent the branch to see
if it would give, ignoring the fresh blood
pouring out of the wound. After a few
minutes of this awkward and pained
movements, the branch split and he was
able to free the section attached to his hand.
He let the Good Samaritan help him out of
the car. Tony wrapped his hand in his
jacket and applied pressure to stop the
bleeding. It was not until emergency
services arrived and he gave them
Susanna's information that Tony finally
passed out from either exhaustion, shock or
both.

When he woke up he was in a
hospital room. There was a dull throb in
his right hand and an IV in his left arm. His
body was sore but Tony managed to lift up
enough to look around. Javier was

standing at the window and Susanna was talking to a nurse.

"*Hermana*?"

"*Dios* Antonio!" she exclaimed making Javier jump.

The nurse came to his bed as well. "Señor Garçia-Torrés, how are you feeling? Are you in pain?"

"Well Señora, I feel like I was in a car accident, my hand hurts like hell and I am sure I missed a date with my future wife."

"Tony," his sister warned.

"Señor, on a scale from one to ten, what is the pain level in your hand?" the nurse refocused him.

Tony shifted in the bed to sit up, "My body is sore, so about a two or three. My hand is about an eight, which I will take considering I had a small branch through my hand which protected my handsome face."

The nurse finished checking his vitals, "*El doctor estará aquí en momentos.*"

Susanna started in as soon as the nurse left, "What happened? Did you drink before you left the house?"

"No, I think somebody hit me but I never saw a thing," Tony sounded dumbfounded, "it all happened so fast."

"Well the authorities wanted me to call them when you woke up. The car was a mess, as it was wrapped around a tree," Susanna walked over to Javier and held his hand.

The doctor came in, "Dr. Arvendondo. Señor Garçia-Torrés, I am glad to see you are awake and talking. That was quite the accident you survived. Do you remember what happened?"

"I was just telling my sister I don't really know. I was setting the car's Bluetooth to my phone and it felt like something hit the car. I was so busy trying to keep the car on the road that I did not notice anything else," Tony shook his head.

"Well here is the bad news, you will be sore for a few days. I will give you pain killers and muscle relaxers. The good news is that you were so unprepared for the crash that you did not tense up which saved you from whiplash. You did a smart thing by leaving that piece of branch in your hand. We were able to extract it without nerve damage. It may give you some problems later, but for now the wound is closed and you have an additional prescription for antibiotics. Finally, your toxicology report came back negative so I can notify the police that no drugs or alcohol were involved." Dr. Arvendondo unwrapped Tony's hand to check for bleeding. "Keep this area clean and dry during showers. The staples will dissolve in a week or so. Stick to the home instructions you will get upon being released and see an orthopedic surgeon in six to eight weeks. The nurse will go over everything at discharge."

Susanna asked, "Is there anything we need to do beyond making him comfortable?"

"Make sure he gets rest and limit the use of his right hand," the doctor shook Tony's left hand, "*Usted es un hombre afortunado. Tener cuidado.*"

As Tony started to rise he asked his sister, "Did you call Richard?"

"Not yet."

"Well we need to keep this between us until they get back," Tony warned.

"But-"

"Susanna, *por favor*. We will not ruin their honeymoon," he said sterner than before. "Don't make me call in that favor you owe me."

He eyed Javier.

"Fine," Susanna led Javier out of the room as Tony picked up his clothes. "Call your date. The police contacted her trying to call the person you called last. This was one hell of an excuse to miss your first date."

10
Revelations and Revenge

Iroh was back on the job. He picked up Richard and Mychal from the airport when they returned from their honeymoon. Mychal was fond of Iroh, but he was just a reminder that the situation at home had not changed. Thailand was one of the best times of her life. Though pregnant and unable to drink the native spirits, Mychal made sure Richard had the best time once he was away from the troubles of work. They relaxed by the ocean, toured the city sights, danced at night and made love in the mornings.

On Richard's thirty sixth birthday, Mychal surprised him with a solo zip line trip through the forest. Afterward they got a *Garra rufa* spa treatment. Both were fascinated with how the tiny fish that were part of the treatment felt like tiny pinches on their toes. For dinner they went on an evening cruise where they dance until after midnight. Once they were back in their villa, they talked until sunrise, enjoyed pleasing each other, and spent the next two days sleeping on the beach. On the car ride home she saw a little of Richard's joy slip away as the corners of his mouth turned down as they passed Rafael's villa on the way to their home. Iroh said very little but his very presence conveyed nothing changed in their absence.

The house was quiet so Mychal immediately checked on Solomon. Richard got an update on any events that happened from Iroh as soon as his wife was out of earshot. She walked around with her dog feeling glad to be back in the comforts of home. Mychal wandered to the back of the property to Susanna and Tony's apartment. She had not been in their space since before the remodel and was anxious to see the changes. Mychal knocked on the door and waited. After a few seconds she tried the door which was unlocked. She entered into a great room divided by a fireplace. Mychal noticed the sienna and ecru oversized chairs on either side of the couch. All three faced a huge wall mounted television.

She noticed the dining area had an aquarium. Living area forgotten; Mychal was quite taken by the tank that also covered one wall and its ornamental fish. Beside the aquarium there were instruments that included a tall bongo with a set of maracas and a guitar hanging on the wall. Past the dining room table was the kitchen and sunroom, which gave a perfect view of the pool and pool house.

As Mychal walked back into the living room, movement caught her eye. She did not notice the blanket on the sofa before. Her heart started to beat. Her hand went to her ankle by instinct only to remember her baton was in the bedroom. Damn! Looking around Mychal saw a lamp she could throw and mentally made an escape route. A cell phone ringtone broke the silence. Tony bolted upright, groping for his phone.

"*¡Hola!*" He paused, "Have I seen Mychal?"

The sleep fog ebbed from Tony's brain. He looked around and saw Mychal holding the lamp. "Yeah, she's here. I think she might be trying to hit me with a lamp or just moving it. I hope she is moving it because I do not need any new injuries this week. I will escort my ninja doctor sister-in-law and redecorator back to the house."

When he disconnected the call she noticed his hand wrapped in a bandage. Putting the lamp down she asked, "What happened to you?"

"I was in a car accident last weekend," Tony slowly got up.

"What? Why didn't you call us?"

"You were on your hon-ney-moon. Mychal, for once you and my brother deserve a break from your daily lives," he waved off the notion.

"Can't argue with that. Car totaled?"

"Not sure yet. The insurance company is still assessing the situation. The Porsche was not new but it might take twenty grand to fix it."

She gave him a weird look, "Why were you driving my car? You could have wrecked your own. Now my favorite cream colored dream is gone."

"If you must know my car was at the dealership. Something electrical under the hood. I was on the way to meet the señorita that helped me with my car and impressed me with her smarts," he slipped on his shoes. "I wanted to surprise her with a drive after our date."

"Did you?" she asked.

"Didn't I just say I wanted to surprise her but was in an accident?. I will tell you about it on the way to the house. If

I know my brother, he is starting to get worried about you."

At the house Tony had to recount the whole story to Richard, even showed him and Mychal his stitched up hand. Richard asked had he been drinking. Tony could only shake his head at his brother's remark and answered he was just in a hurry to meet his new friend. Mychal teased him about dating a woman who was more than a cute body. His brother could not hide his smile at his wife's teasing.

After dinner, Richard came to see their apartment while Mychal called Reese. Richard liked the set-up of the apartment and told Tony so as he got up to leave.

"Richard wait, there is something I need to tell you." Tony pulled out his cell phone and handed it to his concerned looking brother, "The car might be totaled but the authorities have not released it to the insurance company."

"*Policía*? But Mychal said you lost control-"

Tony interrupted him, "I know what I told Mychal and Susanna. I don't want to alarm them. A few days after the accident I remembered new details and told the police. There was a black truck that I glimpsed in the other lane while I was spinning out. I thought it was actually stopped in the road. Strange thing though, its lights were off in the dark rain. When the car ended up on the tree I did not see the truck again. When I told the police, they confiscated the car. Look at these pictures."

Richard scrolled through the other pictures Tony had in his phone of the car. The driver's side rear quarter panel had black paint streaks on the cream colored car and black in the dent on the driver's side bumper. He spoke in an incredulous tone, "What did the authorities say?"

"That they think somebody tried to run me off the road. It was no accident."

Though he said nothing, inside Richard's heart sank.

The third summer session began two weeks after they returned from Thailand. Against Richard's stern words Mychal continued to teach. She argued that sitting home in a fortress would not make her any safer. They agreed she would work on two thesis committees, meeting with students individually. Mychal would be home two days a week by early afternoon. Two days she would remotely teach the thesis seminar. Richard decided that was not enough for him, so he altered his schedule to come home early a couple of days a week. Mychal developed mixed feelings about the arrangement. Some days she enjoyed Richard being home, other days he was brooding and hovering.

Boredom and anticipation drove Mychal to talk with her family more frequently. She called her mother to chat about baby things. She made sure to talk with her brother Max to keep abreast of the fraud situation back in the states. He reported he was working to clear her name while the feds worked on collecting more evidence to support their case against Jacob and possibly her. Before it got to the feds wanting to further investigate her, he became her power of attorney and had a certified public accountant go over her tax returns for the years she was in business with Jacob. Max encouraged Mychal to concentrate on the baby and inquired about their honeymoon.

She gladly switched subjects telling him about their wonderful time and Richard's zip line adventure. Before hanging up her brother asked about the situation with the security. Mychal could only say they were still around so then nothing had changed. With kind words to pass to Richard, they disconnected the call.

The weekend passed quietly and Monday saw Tony returning to work. Mychal wanted to spend time hanging out with Susanna and getting to know Javier. She teased the young girl about their seriousness when she caught up with her later in the week.

"Did I see Javier leaving again this

morning?"

Susanna blushed, "Yes. Last night he cooked the best seared Ahi."

"Seared Ahi?" Mychal was impressed. "Why didn't we eat at your place last night? We just grilled chicken and had a salad."

"Well I want to come up and hang out sometimes, but you know my brother. His attitude can put people off and I want Javier to continue to hang around."

Mychal shot her a mischievous look, "Oh, Javier is not going anywhere. Assuming he has spent the night . . . with you . . . in your bed. I'm just saying."

Susanna could only shake her head, "Are you asking or insinuating?"

"Both!"

"Quit being an *abuelita intrusivo*."

She continued to tease, "You did not say no . . . so was it great? Was it hot and passionate?"

"Mychal!"

The pregnant woman burst into laughter making Susanna blush harder, "I'm just joking. I like him for you. I am sure Richard will too once things settle down."

"He will not have a choice," Susanna ignored the surprised look on the other woman's face. "Don't even ask because I am not pregnant. You can have that. Javé and I are talking about rings."

"Oh shi-"

"Mychal!" Susanna cut her off.

"I mean wow," Mychal hugged her,

"this thing is real. He really is the one."

"Yes I think he is."

Mychal made a face, "When are you going to tell Richard?"

"Maybe tomorrow, maybe next week. I am in no rush. I want the proof on my hand for my brother's sake. Javier has a gala he is picking wines for tomorrow night. He wants to take that money and buy a ring before the end of July."

"Need my help?"

"No, I want to do this on my own," Susanna stood up a little straighter.

"I am here if you need me."

She smiled back at Mychal, "I know, but some battles I need to fight on my own."

After leaving Javier Friday evening before his gala, Susanna had to track down Richard. He was not at home but at the office covering for Tony. She let herself in trying not to startle her older brother. He looked up and smiled, "What are you doing here?"

"I was out with Javier and decided to stop by," she sat on the office couch.

"How did you know I was here?"

"Tony. He texted me to ask about what wine to order; again trying to make an impression on his new girlfriend. When I asked why he was not at work, he said you took his late meeting."

Richard nodded, "I decided he needed some real time off. Since Monday he has been working extra hours to catch up on the time he missed during his accident. I told him to take it slow, but he insisted he wanted to get through the new information security had on the terminated workers."

"Find anything new?"

Richard leaned back in his chair, "One possible lead, but it can wait until Monday. I told Tony that when he called after the meeting. I also told him to enjoy his date. He seems pretty sincere about this one."

Susanna took a deep breath, "He's not the only one."

"Really?" Richard raised his eyebrow.

"Yes, I love Javier. I think he is someone I could wake up to every morning."

Richard said nothing at first. After a few moments he calmly said, "Did you tell my wife?"

Susanna rolled her eyes, "Of course. She walked me through talking to you this afternoon when I dropped off a tennis ball for Solomon."

"Do not encourage her and that dog."

"It was not my idea. Javier and I were walking along the back wall and he found it. I told him it probably came from Rafael's tennis court since that wall is closest to that part of his property. We have found stranger things thrown from his side of the wall when he was younger. Like the steering wheel Rafael was hiding from his mom. Hiding my ass."

Richard was not listening. The hair

rose on the back of his neck and suddenly his mind was clearer than it had been in months. It was like the pieces of a puzzle finally coming together in his racing mind and the finished picture was horrifying. Suddenly the color drained from his face and his stomach felt like a black hole. Damn he picked the wrong time to let his guard down. He called the guards on duty at the house but got a busy signal. He moved and talked at the same time, "Susanna call the police and have them go to the house right now! Call Tony to see where he is in relation to the house and tell him to get back there as fast as he can! I think Mychal is in danger!"

Susanna was dumbstruck, "What?"

Richard already had his keys and was dialing his wife's number at the door yelling back, "Call the police and Tony! Get them to the house!"

He raced down the stairs calling Evan to tell him to get to the house with Mychal. It went straight to voicemail. He dialed Iroh but it went to voicemail too. Richard drove out of the garage like a madman with a sinking feeling in his stomach. He called Mychal's cell phone again hoping to reach her. Getting a busy signal, he dialed the house and got another busy signal. That sinking feeling was telling him something was wrong and it was a matter of life or death.

Standing in the refrigerator digging for a snack, Mychal was frightened when the dog barked. He got up and trotted to her side with ears perked.

"What do you want now boy? No snack for you," she teased.

The dog barked again looking in the direction of Richard's old study. He whined and walked in a circle before issuing two short barks followed by a low growl.

"Richard got you a dog. How cute," Demitri came out of the hallway going to the study. She was dressed in all black with some kind of dark slick stain on her clothes. One of her hands was partially hidden.

Startled, Mychal's heart began to beat faster than racetrack horses, but she willed her voice to sound annoyed, "What are you doing here? How did you even get in the house? What do you even want?"

Demitri walked into the kitchen and the light caught something shiny in her hand. Mychal knew exactly what it was and moved behind the kitchen island. The hair raised on the dog's back and he began barking ferociously. Mychal issued the guard command in Dutch.

"What did you tell him?" Demitri demanded, eyes darting wildly.

"To heel," Mychal reached down as if she were petting the dog, but popped the latch on the baton she kept strapped to her ankle. She palmed it against her wrist, out of sight. "We are just two women having a conversation. There is no need for him to be alarmed."

"Is that what you think this is, a simple talk? We are past that. I tried to talk with you calmly on several occasions but somehow we got interrupted. Oh wait, I forgot you also hit me with a table, threatened me, and slapped me. So thanks to your actions we never had time for a regular woman to woman talk," Demitri's voice started to rise.

"Looks like I'm going to have time at this very moment, so why don't we talk now? What do you need to say so urgent that you broke into the house to talk with me when I was all alone?" Mychal adjusted her position to the end of the kitchen island counter.

"Where do I start? You lied about who you were to get here. You took advantage of Richard when our relationship hit a rough spell. You got pregnant on purpose which made Richard marry you. You fooled this whole family into thinking I was a villain while you were some helpless victim. But worse than anything, you cut Richard off from me," Demitri's bottom lip trembled. "He treated me like I was nothing after all these years of being each other's everything."

Instead of feeling sorry for her, Demitri's speech ignited Mychal's temper, making her forget the other woman was holding a knife. "So because there was a mix up in my name when I was hired for this job that made you a victim and me a villain? You cannot be serious! You pushed Richard away before I even moved here. You cut yourself off completely when you suggested I terminate his child's life. What made it worse was your constant harassment. You just would not leave us alone."

"Liar!" Demitri exploded. "Richard loved me! We did not have time to work through our problems because he was always with you. You or his precious family business. But those things were easy enough to manipulate."

Mychal played dumb, "You manipulated Richard? You wish."

"It was easier than you think," she

smiled at Mychal, "as accidents do happen."

Mychal's temper boiled inside and her emotion reflected in her tone, "**You** were behind all those accidents and the vandalism. Are you crazy, you could have killed somebody. You could have killed Tony. Or Richard."

"Richard was not supposed to be at the docks that day. The rest were collateral damage in my plans." The Greek beauty shrugged, "I could never hurt my beloved. But after that failed mess, Richard increased security and my plans had to change. The only person I wanted to kill was you."

"You would kill a pregnant woman? One caring the child of your so called beloved. You are sick and twisted!"

Demitri made a hurt face then

brought the knife up to level it at Mychal, "Like I said, accidents happen."

"How are you going to make this look like an accident?" Mychal moved from behind the counter.

Demitri moved at an angle to counter Mychal's positioning and to give her a clean line of sight, "Working on it. But I am sure I can figure something out to make sure you perish, leaving Richard and I to raise the child the proper way with nannies and boarding school. I secretly despise kids and would especially hate yours."

Mychal yelled the attack command to her dog who leaped at Demitri and clamped down on her arm growling menacing and jerking wildly. Demitri was caught completely off guard and fell back from the momentum of the dog's weight, slashing blindly in the air and at the dog with her free hand which held the knife. She must have cut him because Solomon let out a loud yelp and released her. Before Demitri could recover, Mychal popped the baton once to extend it and moved into an attack position. With keen eyes and trained precision she moved in just close enough to flick the baton to make contact with the wrist of the woman's non bitten arm. The result was a sickening pop, forcing Demitri to drop the knife and howl in pain as a jagged piece of bone broke through her skin and blood poured out the new wound.

"Shut your damn mouth!" Mychal moved in again this time swinging the baton at the knee closest to her. Demitri howled again. Mychal swung again on the same knee on the opposite side causing the already injured woman to scream in agony as her knee twisted in an unnatural angle.

Then she moved to check on her dog who was on the floor panting and licking his slashed front leg.

Mychal turned to Demitri as she rolled on the floor in sheer agony. "I should break every bone in your body for what you have done. For all the pain and suffering you caused Richard, his family, his workers and their families, and now my dog. You are a vile and repulsive human and I hope you spend the rest of your life in prison with a roommate that trades you for cigarettes."

From the floor Demitri shouted back, "I will never stop coming after you. You and Richard will never have peace as long as I live."

Mychal gave the woman an evil grin and stepped forward raising the baton to attack, "Do you realize there is nobody here but us? Nobody would know what really happened to you. I will tell a convincing story of how I feared for my life and had to defend myself for my unborn child's sake. And as for the time you have left to live, I can fix that problem . . . right . . . now."

"Mychal!" Tony burst into the kitchen. He took one look at the bloody scene and Mychal with the baton raised. He yelled, "*Mi Dios*, don't do it! She's not worth it!"

Mychal stopped mid swing as Demitri tried to cover her head with her dog bitten arm. For a moment the two women locked eyes, one filled with terror as the other reflected rage. Mychal swung anyway too quick for her brother-in-law to react. Her swing was a low one that made a loud clanging sound, sweeping the knife away from the injured woman and over by the dog crate. She spoke to Demitri in a low tone filled with so much hatred that Tony thought it was almost not a human voice, "You almost died today, bleeding and broken on the kitchen floor like trash. Remember *that* for as long as you live."

They heard voices coming from the front of the house.

"*Bella*! Mychal! Where are you?" She heard Richard bellowing as he ran into the kitchen. He took one look at the bloody situation and bear hugged his wife. "*Dios yo no podía lleger más rápido*."

Mychal hugged him back, vaguely aware of all the people now rushing in the house. Feeling like a weight was suddenly lifted, she sagged against him. Richard stroked her hair and kissed it, "It is over. I am here and I have you now *Bella*."

His words triggered something in

Mychal, causing her to tremble. Silent tears freely ran down her cheeks. When he asked was she hurt, she shook her head no. Richard insisted she get checked over by the paramedics. To that Mychal replied to check her dog first. Richard promised they would before taking her baton and leading her outside to the waiting ambulance.

While she was being examined, Mychal saw the other set of emergency personnel loading Demitri into the other ambulance handcuffed to a stretcher by her unbroken wrist. She felt her anger rising again at the thought of all the stress and drama Richard's ex-girlfriend put them through. Mychal wanted to break her other kneecap and some ribs, but remembered the police were there and Richard surrendered her baton. Dammit! Instead when she caught her eye, Mychal gave Demitri a cold death stare and the middle finger.

"Señora Garçia-Torrés?" Mychal
was so angry she almost forgot her name.
She looked around to see who was calling
her name and recognized the middle aged
Filipina woman that she only met once
before. "Detective. . . .Bradford right? I'm
sorry if I forgot your name. I'm beyond
distracted right now."

The other woman gave her an
understanding smile before introducing
herself again as Detective Baird and her
partner Detective Pharr. Richard wanted
them to come back later, but Mychal
wanted to get the questions over and done.

For the next thirty minutes Mychal
answered questions about Demitri and the
incident in the house. How did she get in?
Why did she want to hurt you? Was this
her first confrontation with the perpetrator

since the restraining order was filed? Was this related to the previous incidents involving Señora Salvos? Why was there a signal jammer in the house? The questions continued until the emergency personnel had to leave. The detectives moved with them in the house to finish conducting the interview.

Once in the library, the questions shifted more to Richard and his involvement in the situation. Mychal could see him grinding his teeth, signaling his patience was wearing thin. After close to twenty minutes in the house he said, "My wife and I have been through a lot over the past few months and today was the terrifying end to our torment. I think these questions can wait until mid-morning tomorrow so we can get some rest. Right now I need to focus my attention on my wife and child."

The detectives grudgingly agreed before exiting. As the authorities and investigation unit began packing up, Tony, Susanna and Javier came into the living room to check on Mychal. Her spirits were high but she was suddenly tired. They bid each other goodnight and went upstairs while the others went to their apartment.

Once upstairs the conversation was sparse. They shared a shower with Richard checking over Mychal for any bruising even after she insisted she was not hurt. He left her in the shower, the first time she was alone since Demitri broke in the house. When Mychal finally emerged Richard was waiting with her pajamas. She allowed him to towel dry her hair and braid it, which seemed to relax her.

"Where did you learn to do that and why am I just finding out you have that skill?"

Richard chuckled, "I have a younger sister remember? I wanted to practice a little just in case we have a girl."

"You really want a girl don't you?" Mychal smiled.

He came around and kneeled in front of her. Richard laid his head on her round belly and said, "I just want the baby and mother healthy."

Mychal stroked his damp hair. This felt like a private piece of heaven. The baby moved catching them both off guard. Richard kissed her baby bump and suggested they go to bed. While she slid under the covers, he put away their wet towels. Seconds later he got in bed and pulled her close. Richard told her that the dog trainer called and reported Solomon needed over twenty stitches for his wound but would recover fine. He would be back in a week. Mychal said nothing and instead began to tremble. For the first time that night she started to weep. Richard sat up and gathered her in his arms. She laid her head on his shoulder and cried harder. Her anguish made Richard shed a few of his own tears. All he could do was rock Mychal to sleep whispering words of assurance and love.

11
Festivals and Forgiveness

The weekend was a quiet one.
Monday Mychal went to the doctor for a
check up on the baby. Everything was fine
and the baby had turned into the delivery
position. She and Richard left the
appointment anxious and excited. Security
remained at the house and Richard worked
from home most of the day. When he left
Iroh came to actually watch Mychal. To
make it feel less like adult babysitting, she
taught Iroh how to play various card
games. It made them both look forward to
his upcoming daily visits. Every afternoon

Richard came home his attitude and demeanor got better. He proposed a large festival Friday to celebrate the American Fourth of July and the end of their nightmare.

Friday came and again the lawn was buzzing with people. Richard invited security staff, their families, Mychal's coworkers and their families. Children ran everywhere with water balloons and sparklers, while the adults danced to music from a DJ. As Mychal walked around as hostess, she ignored the dull pain in her back. Despite her previous objections to being part of the hosting duties, she was determined to make sure Richard's party was a success. Thinking it might have something to do with the sandals she was wearing, Mychal slipped into the house to change into sneakers. When she came back, a waiting Richard swept her into his arms and onto the dance floor. Laughing and dancing around with her was the most relaxed Mychal had seen him in months. *This* was the Richard that Mychal fell in love with. He looked ten years younger today with his white cargo shorts and navy shirt. Mychal grabbed his hand and pulled him close for a passionate kiss. The other dancers cheered and clapped.

To signal the end of the festival, Richard had fireworks. They sat hugging as the show began. Mychal sighed and said, "This was wonderful. *Usted es un maravilloso marido*."

"Thank you," he nuzzled her ear. "This was the least I could do for the people who protected the most important thing in my life."

"Awwww," she replied. "They were extended family for a minute. How are

Sifeutes and Mercando?"

"Healing. Their cuts were deep but not life threatening. Sifuetes was here earlier. Mercando could not make it because he is on some heavy pain medication, limiting his ability to drive. They are very lucky considering Demitri's attack on them was so brutal," Richard rubbed her thigh. "Did I mention Solomon will be back on Monday? He has been in physical therapy. I never knew dogs had physical therapy."

"Me either," Mychal made a face and shifted as the dull throb in her back seemed to intensify.

"You okay?"

"I guess. I think this extra thirty pounds is working on my back."

Richard angled himself so he could

massage her lower back, "Better?"

"Yes," it actually was. She let his fingers ease her muscles as the sky lit up before them.

Richard asked the family, Luis and Ruby to stay after everyone left. They sat around drinking wine, watching the fireplace and chatting. Javier was talking with Tony and his new girlfriend Yadira while Luis was showing Susanna something on his phone. Ruby and Mychal watched the crowd, making random comments.

Richard came from the kitchen with glasses and champagne. He handed out glasses then filled each one up. He handed his wife a glass of sparkling apple juice. Richard stood in front of the fireplace to address the small crowd. "Tonight was a celebration. We have much to be thankful for and I am personally thankful for all of you. Together we weathered a difficult and dangerous time in all of our lives. Together we overcame adversity and became stronger as individuals and as a group. To my friends Luis and Ruby, thank you for all your love, support and tolerating my wife and I through our separation. You glued us back together and I will always love you for that."

"*Hijo*, that is what friends are for," Luis responded.

"We love you too dearheart" Ruby added.

Richard raised his glass to salute and they all drank. Then he turned to Tony, "To my brother who stepped up when I needed him the most. You have been my right hand and for that I cannot thank you enough. You even kept my precious wife out of harm's way. All I can do is to make you vice president and chief operation officer of the company. And to your wonderful friend, thank you for helping our family when my brother needed you the most."

Yadira smiled and said, "Somebody needs to keep him straight."

"A promotion and a sexy girl that enjoys keeping me on track, I *will* drink to that," Tony raised his glass and the others followed.

Richard turned to Susanna and Javier, "My little sister is no longer a little girl. She has become a grown, intelligent woman and my left hand. Without you, our wedding would not have been absolutely spectacular nor the estate so beautiful. You really made the magic happen, all while finding a perfect gentleman whose simple discovery of a tennis ball was key to unlocking the mystery of who was hurting this family. Susanna, Mama and Papa would be so proud of the person you have become."

Susanna wiped her eyes and replied in an emotional voice, "I know they would be so proud of all of us."

"You are the true gentleman here," Javier raised his glass to Richard. "You kept your family together in the worst of times. That says much about you. For that I salute you."

The crowd nodded in agreement and took a drink. Susanna hugged Javier.

Finally, Richard turned to Mychal whose eyes were already moist. "To my dear and precious wife. You have truly changed my life. From day one when you walked in this house, I knew I would never be the same. Your larger than life personality swept me up in your world and gave me hope that someone could love me the way I deserved to be loved. Because of you I wanted to be a better man and I will spend the rest of my life loving you."

Mychal wiped away tears as Richard's words touched her heart, "Husband, it is I who am honored to have known a love like yours. Nothing would make me happier than to love you for a lifetime."

A couple of others wiped tears when she finished as well. Mychal blew him a kiss.

"*Saludo*," Richard raised his flute and the group raised theirs as well. After drinking his glass contents in two gulps, Richard cleared his throat to address the group again. "As I said this experience was both difficult and dangerous and I wanted to share with you, *mi familia y amigos*, what has been discovered since my *ex novia* was apprehended."

"Before Mychal moved back in, Demitri was still trying to convince me that my wife was some evil seductress," he winked at Mychal. "She sent texts and called but I refused to communicate. That was why she visited Mychal's office the first time. Once I was told of the visit, I had Uncle Rico get a protection order expedited through the courts. After she was served with the order, the parking garage vandalism started. I did not pair those two events together because I was busy with the fallout from the incidents at work. Even with Tony's help on the shipping accidents, I was still distracted. When she came to Mychal's office again, both the engagement ring and my presence seemed to set her off. Shortly after that campus visit, came the forklift incident that almost blew up the dock. When the authorities became involved, things calmed down a bit. Everything seemed quiet until the wedding incident."

Mychal interrupted, "The wedding incident? Hold on . . . what happened at my wedding?"

Richard looked uncomfortable, "Please *Bella*, do not get upset. I mean nothing really. Demitri came with Rafael as his date. She was arrested and I guess he left. I did not know they were dating because my focus was on my family and their safety. I had not seen Rafael in months and had no idea he was even invited to the wedding. What was found out later was that she moved in with him right next door unbeknownst to us."

Ruby gasped and Luis muttered, "*Mi Dios*."

Mychal said nothing so Richard continued, "Apparently she was watching the house and growing bolder. She somehow managed to get that stuffed animal in bloody baby clothes over the wall. The blood was from Rafael, though I have no idea how she managed to get enough blood from him for that stunt if he was conscious. When the stuffed animal over the wall did not get the reaction she wanted, Demitri got more aggressive. While we were away on our honeymoon, somebody ran Tony off the road in Mychal's car. At first it was thought to be an accident but the police had suspicions after interviewing witnesses and reviewing the evidence. Now they think it was Demitri."

Susanna exclaimed, "What the hell!"

Mychal was speechless. Richard kept his eyes on her for signs of distress.

Tony broke the silence, "I had a notion something was different about the accident. I felt a jarring bump from behind and thought I saw another vehicle while trying to control the car. But things happened so fast, I could not be sure. I had no idea I was hit until the police asked about the black paint on the car's left side and bumper. When Richard came back we talked to the officers that were working with me about the accident. Once they heard there was a series of other accidents, the detective that was investigating the dock incident was notified and he began putting the details of everything together."

Hating to mention the episode with Demitri but wanting to have everything out in the open, Richard finished, "After Demitri came to hurt Mychal the police found a black truck was rented by Rafael except it was not him. He had been tied up in his own pool house for weeks. When the authorities searched the property they found him barely alive. He had been beaten and was severely dehydrated. He's in critical but stable condition at the hospital. He was extremely lucky and is expected to make a full physical recovery."

Mychal interrupted again, "Physical recovery?"

Richard refilled his glass and took a swallow for courage, "Yes physical. No one can say how well he will mentally recover. He has been through his own hell. He too was another one of Demitri's victims. I think we all were in one way or another."

The group sat quiet for a moment. Richard walked over and hugged Mychal.

"Thank heaven it is all over," Luis finally spoke.

"As soon as we find her accomplice or accomplices working for the company it will truly be over and that should be any day now."

"An accomplice?" Susanna asked.

Tony spoke up, "She had help. The incidents on the ship and dock were probably part of her plan but she could not get access to the ship. Nor could she have known what to do to cause such damage. By week's end, Evan and I will have the right person."

Seizing the moment, Susanna said, "Speaking of the right person, I have a confession to make."

Javier held her hand for support seeing her nervousness. Mychal had an idea what she was going to say and felt that she needed to hold Richard's hand for his own support.

Susanna looked around and said, "Javier has asked me to marry him and I said yes."

Ruby and Luis immediately congratulated the couple. Mychal felt Richard's whole body tense then he looked at her with green eyes clouded with emotion.

Javier spoke to the group but looked at Richard, "Being in this whole situation with Susanna and this family made me realize that life is unpredictable. But if you love someone the way Richard and Mychal love each other, that person is worth having in your future. I am sorry I didn't do this the traditional way, but when everything happened so chaotic around here, I didn't want anything to happen to Susanna before I had the chance to ask."

Tony threw in, "Well you did talk to me about it when you asked did I think my brother was going to kill you."

All eyes went to Richard, waiting to see what he was going to say. He squeezed his wife's hand before saying, "While this is not traditional, I understand and agree with your line of thinking. And if you love my sister the way I love my wife, then you have my blessing."

Susanna jumped up and ran to hug Richard, "Oh thank you, thank you, thank you. Mama and Papa would definitely agree."

"I just want your happiness," he hugged back.

Mychal gave her a wink.

The small party went on a few hours more. Mychal's back hurt on and off, but she managed not to show it. Once in bed she asked Richard to massage her lower back again. He was worried and wanted to take her to the hospital.

"No honey, it's not like that. My back is throbbing like an overused muscle. Can't you just massage it a little?" she pleaded.

He complied with her request at first. Touching her plump curves was such a turn on for him. Richard moved from her lower back to her shoulders, kissing her earlobes as he did so.

"Are you taking advantage of a pregnant woman?" Mychal teased.

"Definitely," Richard's hands moved to her enlarged breast barely contained in

343

her thin tank top. He was not satisfied with just touching them. He eased Mychal on her side so he could taste each one without pressure to her back. He trailed kisses from her swollen breast to kiss her swollen belly while he worked her out of her underwear so his finger could stroke what was behind the barrier. Mychal moaned loudly as Richard's fingers coaxed her to the edge of release and his mouth returned to her super sensitive breast.

With ragged breath, he whispered his need. Richard's hands moved up from her center to the sensitive spots in the groove of her hips. Mychal moaned again at his every touch. He skillfully dipped his mouth to kiss the spots his finger left then trailed more kisses across her hips. Richard moved across her to kiss her lower back where he was massaging earlier. His mouth moved to the back of Mychal's neck as Richard joined them. His movements were slow and intense at first while his palms rubbed her overly sensitive breast. Richard's hips rocked Mychal skillfully causing her to shiver with pleasure again and again. He held her close and made deep rocking movements a few times before lying still against her. She made no attempt to separate them but instead lay her head on his arm for a pillow.

"That was the first time we have been intimate since the incident at the house," Richard said into her hair.

"Yeah, I know," was all Mychal said, wondering was their intimacy the reason the pain in her back was now gone.

"*Bella*, do you blame me?" he asked quietly, "because I think I blame myself."

Mychal turned so she could look

over her shoulder at him, "Why?'

"I think I should have handled her earlier. Been more stern or nasty as hell or something," Richard's voice reflected his exhaustion.

Mychal knew there was more behind tonight's emotional speech than just showing appreciation to his friends and family. She pulled his arm tight around her mid-section before saying, "Honey, I do not blame you nor should you blame yourself. Your ex-girlfriend has a few numbers missing from the crazy clock. Period. There were a thousand outcomes that could have happened and nothing you did or did not do could change that fact. You took the right actions at the right times. The only thing I think you could have done different was tell me she tried to crash my wedding."

"I know, but I was not going to let

her upset you and ruin our day. I know you. You would have tried to beat her up, pregnant, wedding dress and all." Richard smiled at the image in his mind.

Mychal chuckled at the image his words detailed in her head. "You're damn right. I would have beat her ass right then."

Richard chuckled too, "See, I made the right call for you. But the arrest might have been her tipping point."

"Honey, who knows? Again you cannot second guess crazy. Let it go. Nobody blames you. Things happened like they were meant to and I finally got to give her a good old fashion back in the day neighborhood beat-down. One that I thoroughly enjoyed. But some broken ribs would have made it better," Mychal finished with emphasis.

"Okay killer, settle down," he kissed her neck. "Your feistiness is turning me on."

"Well sir, since this seems to have taken away the pain in my back, you're going to love what's next," Mychal said before switching positions where she could tease and please him one last time before they both dozed off exhausted.

When Richard signed them up for a labor and delivery class on Thursday, Mychal was surprised. During class she tried to show enthusiasm but was really bored. He seemed engaged so Mychal did her best to put on a happy face. What really made her smile was Iroh trying to be incognito in this situation. Amazingly he ended up being partnered with a woman whose husband was suddenly called out of town. Damn, he was good.

Secretly she was over being pregnant and started her mental countdown two weeks into her last six weeks. Her body had adjusted well during the whole pregnancy, only gaining a little over thirty pounds. She managed to stay fit by walking the dog or doing small daily tasks to keep her active. Only in the past week was Mychal uncomfortable. The pain in her back came and went, sometimes strong enough to make her sit down. Sometimes it was just a constant dull throb. Her doctor said it was Braxton-Hicks contractions and indicated she was almost ready to deliver.

That night after class the pain in her back was so bad she walked across the hall to Richard's new study and said, "Honey, I think we need to go to the hospital."

Richard's face was somewhere between shock and joy, "Okay *Bella* are you dressed?"

She nodded.

"I will get your bag and help you downstairs." Mychal could tell he was excited. Richard looked at her and said, "Don't panic."

That was the silliest thing Mychal had ever heard. She laughed all the way downstairs. Richard's driving wiped the smile off her face. He drove the Aston Martin like a drag racer all the way to the hospital. 'Don't panic' was all she could mumble as she walked into the emergency room. Within minutes they were upstairs in labor and delivery with her hooked up to monitors and him calling family.

By midnight her pain was mostly

gone and they were sent home with no baby and Mychal dilated two centimeters. Disappointed and tired, Richard drove home while Mychal called the family to report the false alarm. Both keyed up and tired at the same time, Mychal made breakfast and afterward they tumbled into bed fully clothed.

The next day Mychal got a call from Max.

"Is my big brother calling to check up on me?" she teased.

"No Richard already called me. He is so excited and nervous. I think I have talked to him more in the last eight months than most of my clients in my seven years of business. Sis, again, you finally got it right with the perfect match for you," her brother teased back.

"I know and we have been through so much. He, no, we deserve some happiness."

"Well I have a little good news. The tax lawyer buddy of mine went over your returns for the years you were in business with Jake. He contacted the Internal Revenue Service and the federal prosecutor assigned to the case. It looks like you are going to have to pay back half the money he borrowed or some percentage of it. Since you paid taxes on the profits already, there is no problem there. But sis, we are talking about a quarter of a million dollars or less," Max sounded sketchy.

Mychal was floored, "He borrowed all that!"

"I guess, but until the investigators can sort through it, the total he lied about was half a million. It is hard to tell whether that was the total of the profit he made or the total amount he got from the government scam. Nothing is definite. You were smart to keep all your records on the partnership and getting out after only two years," Max tried to sound encouraging. "It also helped that the records you had showed you invested your own money and the first year you only got fifteen percent of his total profit, which by the way he lied about."

"What?" she was shocked again.

"Your brother-in-law was really working everybody. He put some of the profits in his nephew's name in a junior account. He set up shell companies and accounts too. It was a colossal mess. So far you and Riley will probably get fines and have to pay back some of the money." Then he added, "No jail time though."

"Damn him! How in the hell did he work it out so Riley got in trouble too?" her mind raced. That kind of money could wipe her out, houses and retirement included. Her sister did not have that kind of money either. Jacob made Riley a housewife and told her his wife should never work. "Where is she going to get money to pay anything back? Riley can't even balance a checkbook."

"I know," Max sighed, "but something will work itself out for her. Let's wait until everything is out in the open before we start to worry."

Mychal was relieved at the news but angry. She did not show it while she talked to her brother about other things at home. She later shared her telephone conversation with Max while watching TV with Richard. His only comment was, "So you will be spared the trial?"

"Yes. I still might be teleconferenced in for some things. It depends on if there is even a trial. If Jacob takes a plea deal, all that would be avoided. Who knows with him," she looked distant as if deep in thought. "I just want him to think of Riley and the family. He has been selfish enough."

"*Bella* that is not a worry for you right now. I am just glad we can possibly avoid two trials," he rubbed her swollen feet.

"Two trials?" Mychal was bewildered at first. Then she remembered, "Oh I forgot about Demitri's trial. Honey, that's about three years away."

"Maybe, but it is a high profile case. It can take anywhere from a year to four years just to hear the evidence in her case. She has already had her initial appearance and after hearing the evidence the authorities presented, the judge ruled she should remain in custody or *prisión preventiva*. Now the detectives are just building a stronger case based on the evidence and there will be a trial with three judges or *Audiencia Provincial*. She can ask for a trial by jury, but that may take longer. Two years was the window I was given," Richard never took his eyes off the television. He really did not want to give his wife the impression that the whole situation was still bothering him.

"So she will not get out even on bail?" Mychal asked skeptically.

"No, she is a flight risk being a citizen of another country," Richard gave her foot a little squeeze, "Don't worry, she will never bother us again."

"I know. Because next time I will

break all the bones in her body and no one will stop me," Mychal frowned.

Richard leaned over and pecked her on the lips, "Easy killer. It is comforting to know I married an American ninja that happened to be a seductive Amazon warrior too."

She sat up and pulled him closer, "You better believe it. Think you can take this American ninja seductive Amazon warrior?"

"Oh no," Richard tried to pull away, "the last time we did that you ended up in a hospital bed hooked up to monitors. *Lo siento niño.*"

Mychal ignored his protest and gently pushed him down on the sofa while working on getting off his jeans, "You know as well as I do, it was worth it.

12

Contractions and Confessions

Richard hit the snooze button before the alarm could wake his wife. He rolled over to see that she was gone. Again. Slowly getting out of bed he started the same task he had been doing for the last week, finding where his wife decided she was comfortable enough to sleep. Sometimes she was downstairs on the sofa with the television on and the dog at her feet. Once she was sitting up in his office chair asleep. This time Mychal was on the sofa in their suite area, fast asleep sitting up. Richard knew her back was bothering

her as it seemed to be the focal point of
most of her contractions. He pulled the
blanket up over Mychal and went to fix
breakfast. Not only was she sleeping
everywhere for comfort, she was eating
every two hours. Quietly, he slipped out of
the room hoping not to wake her.

After breakfast, Mychal went back to
sleep. Richard sat in his office still cleaning
up the financial mess Demitri's sabotage
left. While insurance covered everything, it
resulted in a higher premium for the
company. For the first time ever their profit
margin was down by double digits. While
this troubled Richard, he was willing to
pass the profits down to the workers and
support staff. Mychal would never know
any of this information. He just wanted her
to focus on recovering after the delivery
and adjusting to being a new mom. He was
trying to shift monies within the budget to

offset some of the losses as well.

Mid afternoon while Richard was walking the dog, Mychal came out to spend some time with him. She was moving very slow in an obvious uncomfortable waddle. Dinner was lively and followed by their usual walk in the gardens, hoping to trigger her delivery. After a little nightly television, both fell asleep.

"Richard," Mychal shook him out of his sleep sometime later, "I think my water broke."

The fog in his brain quickly cleared and he looked up at her standing over him, "When?"

"Just now on my way to the bathroom."

He was up and asking questions, "Contractions, how far apart? Is your bag still in the baby's room?"

"I need to change and get this stuff up," she was already back in the bathroom putting a towel down over the slick spot in the floor.

Richard snatched on a t-shirt and pulled on the closest jeans, "Mychal leave that and get on some dry clothes."

"No, it's nasty and I heard it stains," she was not listening.

"If I finish this, will you change please?" Richard hustled her out of the bathroom to get dressed. He threw down more towels before checking on her, "Contractions?"

"Somewhere around ten or fifteen minutes I think," she gave him a nervous smile.

"Let's go *Bella*," he herded her to the stairs after grabbing her hospital bag.

They stopped in the garage so Mychal could catch her breath. Richard held her hand and softly talked to her as he eased her in the truck. Making sure she was secured in her seat, he drove them to the hospital. They pulled over once for another contraction. Again Richard held her hand while his thumb made circling motions above her thumb. He softly encouraged her to breathe and slowly counted to ten during the contraction. Once back on the road to the hospital Richard let out a breath, hoping it would relax his nerves.

"Where did you learn that hand trick?" Mychal asked.

He smiled, "I have been doing my homework."

She managed to laugh, "The internet?"

"Of course. Did it work?"

"A little. I just love it when you hold my hand," she teased.

He shook his head in amazement that she could crack jokes at this time.

In their car trip Mychal's contractions went from twelve minutes to ten minutes. At the hospital she refused to go upstairs until Richard returned from parking the truck. He could not be upset given her eyes conveyed her anxiety. Upstairs in labor and delivery, the staff got Mychal into a hospital gown and hooked up the necessary monitors while Richard called their families. When he came back in the room his wife was clearly relieved at his presence.

Richard went to her and kissed her forehead, "Hey looks like you are ready. Contractions?"

"Less than seven minutes. I am waiting on the epidural," she held his hand.

"What happened to all natural? What happened to 'I got this without any medication," he smirked at her.

"That was before now. So if you ever want another child you will stop teasing and hold my hand through this."

Richard gave a little laugh, "Like I said where is the guy with the big needle?"

Richard received several calls and texts while waiting for the anesthesiologist. When she came in the room and introduced herself, Mychal visibly relaxed. While the staff explained the process, she breathed and squeezed Richard's hand. The staff prepped her back and through inserting the needle Richard kept her focused and talked to her as a distraction. Once the medicine kicked in minutes later Mychal was calmer and her demeanor was better.

She had little time to explain what it felt like to her husband because the staff was checking her dilation. Richard was getting fearful from the increased activity. He voiced his uneasy thoughts to one of the nurses. She assured him the staff was just getting ready with the delivery so close.

Mychal was talking to Richard about contacting Ruby and Luis when her doctor, Dr. Narine came in. "Hello, I was not expecting this call this morning. The baby is a little early but looks healthy with all organs developed at this point. So I guess it is a great day for a birthday."

Her arrival signaled it was almost

show time. She gloved up and checked Mychal's dilation, "Pressure Mychal?"

"Yes."

"Well resist the urge to push just for a minute. We need to change Richard into a mask and gown before we start," Dr. Narine pulled off the gloves.

At the sink she said to him, "Are you feeling queasy? I need to focus on her and I cannot do that if you have a concussion from passing out in the delivery room."

He gave her a nervous laugh, "I will be fine. I will stay above the sheet this time."

"Good call. Now let's welcome your new family member."

In proper hospital attire everyone was ready. With Richard holding her hand,

Mychal followed the instructions from the nurse and doctor. She pushed down while the nurse counted. When the baby's head was out, the doctor suctioned the mouth and for the first time they heard a tiny little cry. Mychal looked at Richard whose face had tears to match her own.

"Once more Mychal."

Doing as she was told, moments later the doctor said, "Look at this girl with all this curly black hair."

She lifted up the most beautiful thing Mychal had ever seen in her life. The doctor placed the baby on her abdomen and said to Richard, "Okay, dad time for your solo act."

Richard placed his hand on the scissors and cut the cord.

"Mychal, the nurses will clean up

Señorita Garçia-Torrés while I finish here. Once they are done she will be right back," Dr. Narine explained.

Richard kissed Mychal gently, "We did it. We got a baby girl."

She wiped tears, "I know."

They could hear the baby crying and were eager to hold her. But first the medical team attended to the new mom and the necessary after birth procedures. After cleaning the baby and recording her vitals, the nurse brought her over with a pink cap on. Mychal held her while Richard marveled at his new daughter. She stared back at him with bright green eyes.

"Time to go to daddy," Mychal passed her to Richard. He sat down, eyes moistening again.

They were talking softly when Dr.

Narine came to praise Mychal for doing well. With a few words of congratulations she was on to the nurses' station for charting. Mychal was feeling fatigued but livened up when the nurse asked if she wanted visitors. She agreed to let the new aunt and uncle in. Susanna and Tony eased in the room not knowing if the baby was asleep. They were emotional when they saw Richard holding the baby. Both took pictures with their cell phones. Each took turns holding her and taking pictures to share with other family members. Two nurses came in the room, one to get the baby and one to care for the mother. Richard left with his siblings so Mychal could talk with the nurses and they could check her. When he came back she had dozed off, so he stretched out on the chair in the room to nap as well.

A little over forty-eight hours later

Carrigan Alejandra Iban was home with
her family. She breast fed well and lost
very few ounces of her almost eight pounds
before being discharged. At home she ate
every two hours which Mychal and Richard
worked together thanks to a breast pump.
Ruby and Luis came by for a visit days after
they arrived home. They immediately fell
in love with the baby and called her Carri.
Mychal's family video chatted almost daily.
Though an adjustment, this was the
happiest time in her life. Richard was a
great father, doing everything from caring
for the baby's belly button to making her
first appointment a month later.

For Mychal's birthday, Richard
surprised her with breakfast in the garden.
First he was up and taking care of the baby
to let her sleep in. Next, he moved the pool
furniture to the garden while his breakfast
was baking. Between checking on the baby

in her mobile crib and making sure his casserole browned, Richard set up their table to include tablecloth, silverware and fresh flowers. He was turning off the stove when his wife came downstairs.

She smelled the food and said, "Who is in the kitchen with you? Carmen?"

"Nobody," he smiled.

"You did all this? You can cook?" she was skeptical.

"Yes, well I mean I can follow directions on a recipe. There is more to me than using the grill, thank you very much," Richard joked.

"I am impressed," Mychal kissed him on the cheek.

"You should be. I only cook like this for birthday wives who are new mothers,"

Richard smiled shyly.

"It is my birthday, I almost forgot with all the changes we have had around here."

"Well I did not. Hurry up and put some clothes on so you can join Carri and I at our reserved table in the garden," he swatted her bottom.

"You are so good to me," Mychal embraced him and pulled him into a deep kiss.

Richard kissed his wife back passionately, feeling his body respond to her body heat against him. They were less than two weeks into their six week waiting period before they could be intimate again. Resolved, he broke their kiss and said, "You deserve it. Now change please, we are hungry."

Mychal quickly showered and came back dressed. She wandered into the garden where Richard had their breakfast and the baby set up. Mychal approached the table smiling at his handiwork, "This is beautiful."

"Thank you," he got up and held out her chair.

"I can't believe you did all this for my birthday."

"This is nothing compared to my birthday," he reminded her. "While it is not zip lining through the forest, I wanted your birthday to be the first event we celebrated as a new family."

Richard was so sweet, it brought tears to her eyes.

"No crying *Bella*, this is a happy occasion."

She wiped her eyes and explained, "This time last year, I was crying my eyes out because I was leaving my family and moving to Spain. This time I am crying because in one year my whole life changed and now I am beyond happy with my new family."

"How about instead of crying over the past, we toast to the future," he picked up his flute of orange juice. She did the same. "To us, which now includes Carrigan."

"Salute," she touched his glass with hers, "now let's eat. This all looks great and I will be disappointed if the taste is not as good as the presentation."

"Funny. You are a regular comedian on your birthday," he teased then prompted her, "first you have to open your gift."

Mychal looked puzzled until she saw the long box on the corner of the table, "What is it? You know you did not have to get me anything. You have already given me everything."

"Critic. Just open it."

Mychal tore the paper away and opened the box. Inside were three plane tickets. "Where are we going? The baby is too young to travel."

"We are going to New York. When this mess with your brother-in-law is over and she is a little older, we will take you home for a visit," Richard smiled at her reaction.

Mychal was speechless and close to tears again. Richard quickly said, "Please do not cry again. The food is getting cold, then I might cry because all my hard work will no longer impress you."

"Oh sir it will still be impressive, because yet again you have surprised me with another hidden talent," she gave him a wink, "Now I want to see what kind of kitchen skills you really have."

Richard woke up from a nightmare; just another in a series he had ever night for the past three weeks. Several of the nightmares were about the baby being missing or stolen. His ex-girlfriend was in nearly all of them. In this one, Demitri was in the house and holding the baby. When he tried to approach her she turned into a demon and burned him and his daughter. Feeling like he was in agony, Richard jolted awake, breathing hard. He looked over to find Mychal missing and for a moment panicked. He heard her on the baby monitor humming for Carrigan. After taking a breath of relief he searched the house in a silly move, checking all the doors and windows. Richard actually contemplated calling the jail to make sure Demitri was still in custody but then remembered it was the wee hours of the morning. He went back upstairs and watched Mychal burp the baby.

"What are you doing up?" she yawned.

"Just checking on my two favorite girls," Richard smiled trying to calm his inner turmoil.

"Well your daughter is asleep and I am coming back to bed when I put her down."

"I will be waiting," he went back to bed but not to sleep. His mind raced trying to figure out a way to put an end to his nocturnal torment. Once Mychal got into bed, he pulled her close feeling some comfort in her closeness.

The next day Richard actually went to work. He wanted to meet with Tony and his security head for an update. They had narrowed the list of people suspected to have helped Demitri to three people whose names Richard did not recognize. Frustrated at the slow progress he made a silent decision that he hoped would help this process out. He was not going to tell anyone, especially his wife.

It took a week for Richard to get some things in order and get his mind centered. He sat in an interrogation room feeling his temper igniting when Demitri hobbled in on crutches as graceful as she

could with a cast on her arm and leg as
well. Richard stared at her blankly.

She sat down ungracefully and
smiled back at him, "Hello love."

For a split second Richard thought
this was a bad idea. He could feel his
temper simmering and was not sure he
could carry the whole plan out. He had to
do this if he and Mychal were to ever have
any peace. Plus he was sure the detectives
would save her before he could choke her
out. They would both be in jail for
attempted murder. Swallowing his anger
he slowly replied, "Demitri."

"What can I do for you today? Have
you come to your senses and dropped the
charges?" she was all pleasant and
business, which made him put his hands
under the table. He wanted to hide his
clenched fist, evidence that he wanted to

choke her out even more.

Calmly, Richard said, "I came for two reasons: one, I came to talk about us and two, for some understanding or clarity to help both you and me."

Intrigued she leaned forward, "Go on."

He took a minute before saying, "Remember when we broke up the first time. It was a disaster for us both. The dramatic fighting and destruction was drawn out unnecessarily. It finally ended when you wrecked my first Range Rover and tried to have me arrested claiming I attacked you."

"Yes, that was a terrible time. I think we were both hurt and wanted to hurt each other. In the end I apologized and recanted my statement," she pouted, "and you said you forgave me."

"I did but things were never the same. We both knew that."

Demitri sighed, "You are right, they were not."

Richard gave her a sad smile, "We did have a friendship though. That was one of the few things we did manage to salvage."

"With benefits," she added.

"Twice in six months is not a benefit," Richard shot back. "And I had to find out I was not your only benefit through a magazine. Obviously there was never going to be another us, as in a couple."

Demitri gave him a fake injured look, "Again, sorry."

"Of no consequence obviously because I thought we were better friends. I valued your friendship over the surrounding factors," he kept emphasizing the word friend.

"I valued that too," she agreed.

"Then why did you act like a jealous idiot when I started dating again? You were already seeing other people and doing what you wanted to do. Like I said, we both knew there was no chance in hell that we would ever be a couple again. What was the problem?"

"Because she was not right for you!" Demitri practically yelled. "She was all American and uncultured. She was not refined and poised."

Richard sharply said, "She was not you."

"She was nothing close to me and you were too blind to see that," she spat out as if the notion was a bad taste in her mouth. "All you saw was a party girl in a bikini. She had no proper lineage and name. She used you and took your hospitality for a weakness to end up in your bed. And you fell for it like some wounded animal that wanted some caring attention."

"You make it sound like another time I remember, when I was grieving my parents and someone took advantage of that moment," Richard eased out.

Demitri ignored his pointed comment, "I understood you had needs and she was a means to an end. But the pregnancy and the marriage were just as you said, the act of an idiot. All that even after I exposed her."

He sat back in his chair, "You did not expose anything. I already knew she was in trouble back in the states."

"She used you!" Demitri slammed her good hand on the table. "She lied about everything! I could not get you to see that the more time you spent listening to her lies, the more you were trapped. So I decided to help the person I called my friend before it was too late."

Richard gave her a puzzled look, "Help me? How could anything you did be considered help in any way? Was part of your so called brand of help destroying my car and wrecking my family's business? Please explain to me how those things could have possibly been considered help."

Demitri's whole demeanor changed, "You would not leave her side unless for work, so work became a little more consuming. For once you were more focused on your life and not hers. She would see how your business was more important to you than her. She would leave you-"

"Demitri you almost killed people at the dock! Myself and Tony included! How would that have worked out in your master plan if I was dead?" he exploded.

Demitri sniffed and said, "That was not my idea. You were not even supposed to be at the dock that day."

"So that was not your idea but the rest was? Vandalizing my car, crashing the wedding, almost killing my brother, and the teddy bear was all an attempt to garner my time? And Rafael agreed to all that, all those incidents to get the attention of your ex-lover?"

"He was just a pawn whose sex was better than yours. It was easy since his ego was bruised after Mychal beat him up in response to his attempt to seduce her. It gave him a confidence boost to have the better woman in his bed. The woman Mychal could never be anything close to. Everything was great until the wedding. He got me out of jail then accused me of using him. He tried to throw me out of the house and I simply could not have that," she finished in an indignant huff.

"So you beat him with his own golf club to the point that he is still in the hospital. Why?" Richard was more disgusted than confused.

"Because he was in my way! He threatened to expose me. And I still had so many things to handle."

"Things like terrorizing my wife and

threatening my child. I knew that stuffed bear over the wall was you," Richard raised his voice.

She rocked back in her chair, "It seems your wife cannot take a joke."

"A joke? Is that what you call attacking her with a knife?" he sounded incredulous.

"I just wanted to talk, to tell her to leave with or without the baby. I needed the knife for protection. The last time I confronted her she hit me," Demitri returned his awed look.

"I guess the joke is on you because she is still my wife and your little talk ended with broken bones. No more dancing and theater for you," Richard gave her a wolfish grin.

Her face clouded and turned

crimson. Demitri snatched up her crutches, struggled out of her seat and knocked on the door to signal the guard. She turned to Richard, "This chat is over."

"Do you want me to tell Gustav you said hello?" he chided.

"Who is that, your son? What an ugly name for a child." Then she added, "Your tasteless wife must have picked that name out."

Richard smiled, no longer masking his emotion, "Goodbye Demitri and thank you."

She turned back supported on crutches and asked, "What are you thanking me for?"

His reply was, "Your understanding and cooperation."

Demitri's exit was not her usual dramatic gracefulness, but awkward and assisted by the guards. When she was gone, Richard let out a deep sigh and his shoulders sagged. Slowly he exited the room.

The case detectives were standing outside the door. One of them asked, "Are you okay Señor Garçia-Torrés?"

"I will be as soon as you tell me that you recorded all that," Richard raised his eyebrow.

"Yes sir. Your little conversation is what we needed to have an airtight case for all the other charges. She basically confessed to everything," Detective Pharr confirmed their plan worked.

"And that last comment helped?"

Detective Baird spoke up,

"Definitely. Now that we know who was not her accomplice, we can put pressure on the two we think that might be until one of them breaks. We will say she confessed and included their part in everything to see which one wants to plea deal out."

"Keep me posted and thank you," Richard shook hands and turned to leave.

"We should be thanking you Señor Garçia-Torrés," the male detective assured him.

"That was a necessary evil to make sure Demitri never gets out of prison. The fact you made this whole meeting happened means for the first time in months, I can sleep without the nightmares," Richard bade them farewell.

That night Richard slept cuddling Mychal. He slept through her feeding the baby. He even slept through his alarm the next morning. Mychal had to wake him up to see if he was going to work. He woke up long enough to tell her he was going to the baby's appointment that afternoon.

At Carrigan's first appointment Mychal and Richard were typical first time parents, asking questions and all emotional when she got her shots. She was very fussy and would only be soothed by her father. After the appointment they picked up takeout and headed home. Between baby feedings Richard flirted with his wife, kissing her neck and whispering words of love. Later Mychal let the dog out for the last time of the night.

A while later she went upstairs to check on her husband and child. She found Richard napping on their sofa holding Carrigan. She quickly took a picture so this moment would last forever. Not wanting to bother them she laid on their bed to catch a nap.

She woke up to the baby crying and saw Richard putting her in the bassinet with a pacifier. He soothed her back to sleep before laying on the bed with his wife. He pulled her close for a tender kiss that turned into a passionate one. Richard whispered against her lips, "You are one sexy momma."

"Oh no you don't. By my count you still have another week," she offered.

"Technically it should be three days. The two days before you had the baby should count toward my six week waiting period. Meaning my waiting period is over . . . now," his hand cupped her engorged breast. "I am so glad you kept this upgrade."

"Honey your post baby math is really terrible, " Mychal teased.

Richard already had his shirt off and was pressing himself against her thigh, "Yes wife, yes it is."

¿FINALISADO?

ABOUT THE AUTHOR

Sean Scott Kerns currently lives in the Hampton Roads area of Virginia. Sean's previous works have been published in the *Rhapsody in Black* magazine since the early 1990s. Her passions include travel and martial arts. The Foreign Engagement is the follow up book to Sean's first novel The Foreign Exchange. Continue to follow Mychal and Richard's escapades in the conclusion of the Foreign Exchange trilogy, The Foreign Endgame, the next book in the series.

Check out her website at

www.seanscottkerns.com